*TABLE OF CONTENTS:*

## AN ELEVATOR IN ISTANBUL

# The Story Of Me: Born Again And Again

I can almost remember being born
Without thinking too hard, I swam out
The canal and those childhood days when
Everyone was still around
Needed them to carry me around

***Time passed***

We'd play on the sidewalks
Jump rope and tag, musical chairs
Cousins and friends
We danced; knew all the steps
We'd write down the words so
We'd sing the songs well
Barrels of wine in the cellar
That wonderful smell
Mexican hat dance, the polka
Tarantella watch out
New year's parties and favors
No one ever wore out
Every Sunday was a holiday with
A family so large
Easter candy, Christmas presents
Made for a wonderful surprise
Birthday parties always special
With the family stopping by

***Rites of passage began***

Confirmation, communion from
A cup, but the blood was forbidden
It would be several years

Before they'd let us sip it up
Wipe it dry with anointed cloth
Wearing stockings with garters and
Being happy anyway as
They seemed to slide down
Nervous laughing, pull them up
Strapped in a girdle, a woman now
I was told; please behave like a lady
I must, thought I was already one of those

***We moved then from the concrete***
No more hot summer nights where
Moms would chant "Time to come in now"
But to an ocean side spot
Known as "the country"
A big house, a heat vent in the floor kind of scary
And a dog in the yard, farm animals next door
Not too much, not too many
Chicks and ducklings
No cow that I remember
But I loved being lost in the sea
Every day in the summer we'd swim
And the cousins would
Visit, big barbecues, we'd play
Long yards, large gardens, fresh seafood galore
The men played pinochle while
Italian women cooked away
Poker betting with pennies is how
My grandfather'd play, kept a jar atop the
China cabinet, exotic dishes, silver forks
I'd hear the men sound off when a
Wrong bet was made like they'd
Lost a fortune all at once, market crashed
Wine flowed, dinner served and
Night never came, every day was the
Longest forever without end

Fall came back and school
Then Kennedy was shot

I will never forget, no I will not
As the earth stood still grieving
In a tight spot, didn't have to understand
No not at all as lives began to fade and fall

### *Next place across from a dairy*

Laid back but in from the beach
Lead the cows to apple trees, feed each one
Her fill fermenting apples making drunk
Kicking heels slurring moos, do they slur?
Streams, fields and cow chips, snakes under rocks
No Sisters of Charity a public school now was
Quite a change for me with a man for a
Teacher these crazy modern times to a
Child of eleven, how will I survive?
We moved from the dairy to the lake
At least there's swimming summer days
And walking round it on summer nights
Barefoot in the rain
Winding roads; lush jungle of trees
Peace, quiet moves in and surrounds, tanning
How brown, love it and the sound of
Bikers rumbling by each spring, to the pizzeria near
My favorite beach, I'm there not a moment to spare

New school new friends new life never ends
More rites of passage in sweet 16 and telegrams from
Home, Uncles, cousins don't roam so much
Life has changed since those days
Grandparents came to stay, graduation coming soon
Never thought I'd see this June

### *Life moves on*

Part of my design a son and new life
I stick around though husbands go
More than one in mistakes to make
Closing in breathing down neck's nape

Drooling over, like my son's chin but I grab my sword
In my arms he's held strong with the other take a swing
I will not give in, no snake mesmerizes off guard
My head on my shoulders, together we stand
See my idealistic ways from Italian family life
But they are right in how they lived, the world not
Up to speed, give another a chance
Learning experiences no purpose, no need
A sister's born, so precious, by my side he now stands
I hold her in one arm strong raise my sword again
We leave this place us three, new life for us somewhere
Will live in hope, it will be

I became professional against all odds and raised grown
Children strong, we laughed, we cried, we stood side by side
I like it and have no care at my old age forever 21
That perfect number holds the key to life, doors open wide
Responsibility all mine no need to age from here
I haven't and I won't, oh my body argues
Time to time but I say remember when
It says yes and on we go to welcome life
Whatever next it holds
Has that time passed forever gone?
No way, not tomorrow and certainly
Not today, my sword still with me
Yet I know enough
About time I say, wouldn't you?
There's still so much to do

---

## *The Short Of It*

*I'm a self-published author of two books, working on a third that I am constantly distracted from by my blogs, flash fiction, short stories and poetry I write.*

*I'm also a TEFL instructor, have lived in a few other countries besides the US, substitute teach at the local school district, and act as the granny-nanny for my grandson. I love walking, cooking, reading, traveling, teaching, learning, language, movies, vampires, mummies, zombies, other assorted creatures of the night, science fiction, romance, action, adventure, classics, Latin, Bushmills 21-Year Old, Chianti, Cabernet Sauvignon, Soave, D'Abruzzo, Ouzo, Sambuca, Bulleit Bourbon, the ocean and tanning.*

# Comfy Clothes, Pajamas But No Bras

***Shaken, On The Rocks: Summer Martini***

Fresh crisp liquid

I savor as elegant stuffed olives work their way

Through crushed ice

To the pinnacle at the bottom of the glass

Crystal frosted etched design

Cloudy, dirty

And another with broken icebergs

Floating

The pile of olives almond filled

Still, sophisticated

I drink and am awakened

I absorb flavors deep

And exhale heady re-freshness

The world sparkles

I shine

A pitchfork swizzle, I spear my prize

The salty cured process

The glass chink-clinks

And I imagine years past

Strapless dresses

Straight skirts and suits

A ceiling fan hums

Cold steam in my eyes

We'll always have Martini

Drink deep, I imbibe

***Rowing In A Third World***

An extended weekend for the border run
What is that, you say
Put your big toe out and bring your big toe in
Over the borderline of your country again, let it begin
New visa, new passport stamp
Another 3 month reprieve so we all can stay
But what do I see when I come back this way

Students in boats for rowing practice
Staring into space, they idly float by
An all-nighter at the club, I'd wager and win
Where energy danced away and went awry
Can't blame them or the one place they can be free

No coxswain nearby but instead
A football field covered in seagulls
Oh turf rest in peace
I shake my head, yes I'm home again
There's no other place this scene can be

No magic carpets really but many carpets are sold

And exotic fabric for quilting 1001 nights
Modern Sultans with cell phones
Pass the poor standing near street-benches texting away
"Double cheese and large fries to the corner I'm at
Teşekkürler, please, without delay"

### *More Border Run Fun*

We met, she told me I'm her first American friend
An historic day for both of us in March, 2010

So personable she is with so much promise
An Engineering student at a competition
Building robots with her team
So much younger than I but together
We were ageless enjoying the town

She'd been here before, a favorite student place to go
And she proudly showed me around to
All the best places to be and enjoy during my brief stay
Representing very well her home country

Everyone around the world should be this way
Differences between us all would be less I can say
Later she left for her connecting train
But we have kept in touch till this very day

I'm sitting at a bistro now like other Europeans
A real part of them I am, through nationalities in me
Next to flower boxes looking across the street
Oops, I don't mean flower boxes looking but me; I'm doing the looking
At the sea

There's a better way to put that I don't doubt. Maybe later I'll figure it all out and edit this piece with my audience unawares. What fun I'm having with blogging-share.

On this street cars fly by
Lending a contradiction to the peace I can't help but feel
Just beyond assorted boats dot the surface, making specs
On the border of the sky
Is that a battleship there, right there, look, straight ahead?

Interesting thoughts occur that this place knows
So much more than me, and that
Everywhere but my country is prepared for anything
Because of venerable experience I know it would be

A few days later back at my favorite café
It's my turn to spend the moments before I board the train
To marvel one last time
At the unique scenery I will leave behind

The Macedonian churches in the middle of buildings
Seeming out of place, but they were
Built there long before these apartments existed
Before there were a trace, and now
Some of which look dilapidated and some are tall

Together they make an eccentric horizon
As if the streets were an elongated desk and the churches
Were paperweights of a monstrous size that are
Anchoring the buildings down, unmovable, strong, keeping leafs
From flying, held in place, tethered against any storm

Like a vision for all time
That will never leave my mind

## *Skinny-Dipping In The Dead Of Winter*

I came into consciousness on the floor. Slowly I managed to get to my feet, look around in the pitch black of what I knew was the living room and drew a complete blank, not remembering where the light switch was or where I'd dropped my clothes. How many times had I been here, why couldn't I find anything fleeted through my mind. Staggering a little I made it to the kitchen and looked out the door window at my house, where my children and his son slept. I'd never liked this arrangement, never liked being separated from them. The night was breathtakingly frozen, the trees covered in ice, the drive in plowed snow, and it was densely cold. I found my way back and put my hand on the arm of the couch to steady myself directly onto my keys. How did they get there? I couldn't remember. Breathing a thank-you I grasped them tight. Not caring about anything else, I firmly positioned the one in my hand that would unlock my door.

The last time we were together as a family didn't end well. We'd come home after visiting friends, his friends, and as we pulled into the drive I'd sighed "don't you wish we could have a long hallway to connect both places so we could reach each other and be together?" "No." He'd said it so flatly. "You dohn-'t?" My voice dropped defeated and cracked through the paralysis that was my chest. My heart moved into my stomach to be digested. I wondered what kind of meat it was as my lower back shot pain through me. He said it again, "no." Why am I standing here at all?

Once I stepped out that door it would slam locked behind me; I'd never be able to wake him. I knew I couldn't drop the key or I'd be stranded, naked, freezing in the cold; what would happen if I were caught. Making my way back to the kitchen, I faced the door, breathed in, opened it, stepped out and ran. I let my body tense forbidding the cold to touch me; my feet didn't slip as if I were a mythical creature of the night that bounded but a few graceful strides to arrive on the front steps. Still not feeling the ground, I slid the key into place, and the door opened onto a vision of children asleep under piles of blankets on the living room floor, my living room floor. With the final stride I entered and slid under with them as the door slammed behind me. No one stirred. My body began to tremble from the shock of below zero; I calmed my breathing and felt warmth begin creeping up from my toes. Although I'd tucked part of the blanket under me so as not to be detected, I drifted off uncomfortably; "what if the kids found me like this" stayed with me as a conscious thought.

I awoke a few hours later, the sun blazing through a window onto my face and no other sounds but the soft breathing of innocents. I rose, put on warm clothes: sweats, a cowl neck sweater, an oversized flannel shirt, my favorite slouchy socks, and walked over to the phone. Better. I had one chance when I called that he'd wake from his stupor and let me in so I could get what was left behind. I felt no effect from the night as I concentrated on each ring. He answered on the third and I crossed the drive. As I gathered things together, surprised how close they'd been to where I'd stood, we exchanged digs about a night I knew he'd never clearly remember. Lord knew I didn't. "Why is there cream cheese on the edge of the counter?' " Don't you remember…?" I cut him off speaking softly, "No." Arms full, I teased a goodnight and left. The children slept peacefully as I made coffee and straightened up around them. "We'll have a taco-burrito fest later if they'd like" was my thought. I walked to the window with my steaming cup and sighed-in its fragrance as I looked out on a perfect frozen morning, stunningly brilliant, intoxicatingly crisp.

***On Mühürdar Caddesi Poe's Alive and Well Near As I Can Tell***

The Ravens rested on the rocks of a lighthouse perch
"Looking more like vultures between the gulls" I thought
While the sun shone strong in my dirty window as I
Reflected on my walk
It's not my place but a benefit they tell me
A perk of my trade giving me a reason to stay

There was one alighted in the tree just outside of me
Another Raven of course and the sun hid
Not on purpose I hope, not on my account, an omen perhaps
The pale blue sky and clouds wait for spring to battle winter
No defining color, that is typical for here I've learned
In two days it's March, one of you make up your mind
Soon, so I know what to wear

Meanwhile my jacket isn't dry; the fan in my room
Makes it seem all the colder outside.

I can see out the window with no sun, but even with it
Should it decide to shine, the Raven's still there.

Cue a flock of Ravens to sail the sky, do they cry evermore
Sure if you'd like, but the seagulls don't mind
Unmoved by all going on, pigeons coo too as
They cover cobblestone, peck scraps here and there,
And get chased by the children, kicked away by adults

Everyone's too busy, even the birds
And unable to give it the time

### ***Didn't Start Out As A Poem: The Check-Out Boy***

One day I went to the grocery store
I needed half 'n half, chips and ¼ lb bats' lips
Yes, I'm serious about the chips
I love 'em with dips, the kind that I make
I stood in the checkout line with customers behind
My turn soon, I approached
The checkout boy beamed excitement
With the happiest face
Looking away from other customers right at me
I was confused needless to say

It was my turn
He could no longer contain
He blurted at last "I know who you are"
"Me?"
"Yes, you were in that movie!"
"What movie?"
"That one with the witch! You're that witch!"
"That witch" I thought "Not a princess, not a handmaiden but a witch
Now why would he think that?"
He told me the name of the movie
And I knew

I drolly mentioned the actress

My voice dropping
Then the character's name, "you think I'm her"
I turned to the couple behind me, ruefully shaking my head
They tried not to laugh, not a very good attempt
He just wouldn't quit "Yes!  It's you! It's your hair!"
"She has to have hers fixed to look like I do
It could be a wig
Mine grows this way
I'm not her" I shook my head no
This is so not fair…

He became serious, and nodded
As he rung my order, a proud smirk on his face
He just knew he knew my secret
I wanted to keep it that way so I could shop free, unknown
I knew he'd tell his friends he'd met an actress
I took my bag and went home

As I put bats' lips in the blender
I heated half 'n half and poured espresso left standing
From the morning, stagnant and strong
I mixed lip frappe, cream cheese, onion soup for chip dip
I put everything on a Libra-zodiac tray
And told the broom, mop and bucket to take care of the kitchen floor
They didn't budge, didn't stare back, but just leaned
Against the utility closet door
I looked around at the mess, later on then I guess
I got comfy on the couch
Shot a glance at the fireplace, so still, so cold
It lit
The button control in a floor panel near where I sit
"That's much better I must say" as
I watched centipedes that crawled stone crevices scurry away

While I watched a classic movie
My mind began to drift
"Imagine him saying I was that witch
Where would he get such a notion?
People think the strangest things

An adage but it's true
Like it or not I made his day
Ah, what can you do"?

Then a warlock blacked out streetlights
Just because he could
"Good trick but a waste", I thought
"There're better things to do
An actress of the big screen he says
No, it's just not true"

***A Paella Western***

*Adapted from "An Apartment In Madrid" a Novella & eNovella*

One evening I was invited to accompany a friend for a night out. Orlando and I were to meet up with his boyfriend and take it from there; with Madrid being open all night long we'd find something to do.

We arrived at the spot, sat for a while and, for whatever reason the boyfriend didn't show, we managed to have a nice time nonetheless just talking. Orlando didn't seem to be all that surprised by the way things were turning out. Between 2 and 3 A.M. I threw in the towel and decided to head home. The next day, as I thought about the evening before, I decided to compose (using the term loosely) a country-western spoof song about my friend being left stranded by his boyfriend in Lavapies, Madrid, Spain:

***Left in Lavapies***

*I was a sittin' on a bench*
*A bench nearby the street*
*Waitin' for my love*
*A love I know's so sweet*

*I waited and I waited*
*But no one ever came*
*In the middle of the night*

*I kept a wishin' his name*

*But he left me, he just left me*
*'Till early that A.M.*
*Just a sittin' and a wishin'*
*The morning my only friend*

*So, I walked home real slowly*
*Feelin' heavy and alone*
*Good thing I live close by*
*Close by and not far to roam*

*Left in Lavapies on a bench by the street*
*As the couples walked by me*
*Holding hands, cheek to cheek*
*Talkin' and a laughin'*
*While some just staggered drunk*
*But I was left in Lavapies*
*He left me there that skunk*
*I was left there on a street bench*
*How much that just stunk*

*Left in Lavapies,*
*Left in Lavapies,*
*Left in Lavapies*
*Relationship's all bunk*

*Left in Lavapies*
*Left in Lavapies*
*Left in Lavapies*
*Whiskey's gone, can't get drunk*

*Left in Lavapies*
*Left in Lavapies*
*He left me, Lavapies*
*Guess I could become a monk*
*Left in Lavapies*

*Left in Lavapies...*

I realize there's no dog that ran away, an important element of country-western blues, but I did get the whiskey in there. In any case not to worry, I won't be quitting my day job to become a composer.

***Excerpts From A Dictionary Beginning With "O"***

***Orgy*** – functionalistic state of multiple realizabilities

***Functionalistic*** – having a purpose physical/mental, mind/mental, physical/mind, mental/mind, physical/physical, mental/mental, mind/mind, unless serving a purpose: ibid and resulting in purpose

***State*** – condition individual and collective, an entity comprised of people inhabiting a specific physical area in nature as in a geologic location, an entity comprised of people of similar mind, an entity comprised of people of similar physical condition, a condition comprised of people who are joined in similar mind, a condition of people disjoined in dissimilar mind resulting in chaos

***Realizabilities*** – inherent natures of people to translate perception to the objective, natural analysis of form (real:genuine/true, eyes:instruments of perception, able:possibility)

***Multiple*** – more than one representation, image, intuition, action (imago, imitatio, admonere) similar to:

***Juxtapostion*** – an alignment (just suppose) using a:

***Quantified Variable*** – the nature of substantial flexibility, of being, versatile integration

***Integration*** – a condition of integrity

# *Stages*

***So Much For Mythology***

I had something else written and I thought it too risqué until I read a painfully long piece of prose about ankles, ankles in boots and I stopped reading, stunned, thinking, "That can't be what they want" they're so reserved, conservative, they say upscale publication, but maybe it's underlying there

What I wanted to say

My Father is dying, Dad, wasting away

At 125 he's developed so much the doctors can't keep track

He'd be on my unit, Skilled Nursing, in a family of multiple train wrecks, not alone, now down to 100, maybe less

We stopped getting along a while ago, he couldn't make me anymore and I thought, "what will I do when you're not here for me to be mad at"

Not really mad just taken aback by

There can never be another, you're one who's unique, there'll never be another you

That song you taught couples to sing at meetings so much like AA, to convince them they should stay married and for what

They found they don't like each other anyway and they know without a doubt, "I'll never find another you"

Shouldn't have found you in the first place – ha, a mutual feeling setting one free

We, together, don't want to find another you, each other, what are you doing here with me

But this is nothing like reading about ankles in boots

So who will it be to cause me to be taken aback

Who will others use to be better than who I portray

It's been a long hard road this life we've had and I can't get distance enough but I know I'll never come across someone like you in the most euphemistic way

If we weren't so alike I'd be free but I'll never find another you because that's me

I never knew someone who hated a parent, not personally, not firsthand

Always examining I looked inside myself and knew I never hated, knowledge is so unfair, I could be surprised and hurt but not for one second was love ever gone or just not there

Nor for less than a second, you might not have made it I'd thought, now that you've passed

The design was quite grand, I crossed the Plain of Lethe and drank deep from Mnemosyne, I knew I accepted
I could remember, even being born

I was sent back by Something greater than us both
A Creator of a masterful plan

But it wasn't necessary I be appeared to, for a secret to be revealed

Nothing mystical really, it had always been clear that I knew the Designer was one to me so dear, who else would it be

I was thinking and it hit me "oh my it was you", my thought following after "how do I tell him" all the things I always knew

I saw it so clear
I put my head on your shoulder and said, "We're ok now, you and me, you know

We really are, I'm sorry I couldn't be there when your time breathed its last"

No retrospect would inspire nor dictate another path
I am whom I am that I know, and of that truth I will never let go

***Romantic Antithesis***

*Have you ever wondered why you did things the way you did, why you weren't stronger, more rational, and clearer in your plan?*

Long ago, my grandmother shared with me some simple truths: wine with a meal is good for you, a cocktail before dinner gives you an appetite, and my favorite: if you put bourbon in your tea you'll never catch a cold (that certainly shines a holy light on bourbon as the sword being pulled out of the stone). Don't stray from these paths, though. If you go overboard with indulgence or combine too many medicines, there will be a price to pay. I paid a high one, one night into day:

I was so hung over driving these roads
With my marriage falling apart

I believed my co-drivers were in
The same condition

Of mind, of soul, of heart
And would never let me crash
They knew, we were connected
In my mind they had to

I went shot for shot in a double shot glass
As each friend arrived uninvited at the news
No one would see reality or if they should have been there at all
Festivities were not about to save our day
We didn't have one anymore, we never did

Presumptuous do-gooders
All friends of the groom, in their honor
I offered sacrifice to a porcelain god
My own

You know the one; although, there may be some who have not and to those: good for you!

How cool it was on my cheek
That pure white rim
One or two came to check, “she’s ok”
No, not when he’d moved out and back in with no key
All in the same day

By the time they were gone, I'd seen peripheral foursomes
"I see four of everything" I had let everyone know
Later on I closed my eyes falling into uncomfortable sleep
That kept my body bobbing, as if floating in the deep

I awoke a few hours later just moderately drunk
Only one of everything, not four
I could handle that, I had to;

There was my job, my responsibility
That no one could tell existed by me

The interstate, bumper-to-bumper at eighty-five mph
Linked us car-to-car and thought-to-thought

As we aided, pushing each other
Down a life-highway to work

Giving space to exit, ease onto a ramp
Then accelerate to fill that empty place

All new friends of the bride I made that day, I thank you
Take that, presumptuous friends of the groom with no sight anyway,

We left no gaps; there was no void
I was complete; yes, I am whole

It became the same message afterward, then day after day until I took control, reorganized and made the change. There was never anything to give up on; I got through the pain.

Hangovers never help you
Trust me, it's true
Without the big headache
I still knew what to do

***Couldn't Knit To Save My Life, But I Can Sew***

She closed the book, placed it on the table, and finally, decided to walk through the door. She pushed back to stand but her mind wouldn't rest. "A third-world country, of all places to choose! What happened to Italy! I never worried. He was safe there." Her thoughts whirred round as she tried to think of grocery shopping on her own. Somehow she'd convince him to leave. She leaned forward again, her hands poised for her next thought, something profound so she could face what was there outside that door. What's that she was hearing?

There were ‘bloop’ sounds in the background so she stopped, let her hands drop and listened. She didn’t know what she’d write anyway and she needed to get out. She picked up her cell and stared at it. It wasn’t any alarm on the cell. “Bl-ll-loop, bl-ll-loop”. What was it? After minimizing her document screen she saw messaging was open. Duh. It was her sister-in-law, well, ex sister-in-law.

“I just got my computer but I have to find out if I have a camera in it and I don't know how. I'll have to ask your nephew. Anyway, once I get it set up I'll let you know.”

“I was typing and I kept hearing these bloops... so I saved and diminished the screen... forgot I had messages open. Couldn't imagine what alarm it was.”

“Bloop alarm - everything talks today. Anyway, so when I find out if I have a camera on this computer... I'm gonna go poke around... I'll let ya know.”

“Yes, that's why it threw me. I don't usually have the volume up that loud anyway… Sounds good… bye.”

“That was kind of crazy”, she thought as she shut down the laptop, “ a disjointed conversation, she’s been trying… hhmmm,” but all too easily she fell back into frustration and how much she wanted him somewhere safe. It was more of an adjustment than she’d ever expected that began her keeping a journal in the hopes of keeping her sanity. “That’s enough!” Out the door she went.

The shelves had American brands intermingled, which helped her figure out what the different products were; figuring out the currency was pretty easy. The girl at the checkout had asked her something but it was lost to the both of them. Someone was found who spoke a few words of English and she understood that the store gave discount cards for sales like in the States. Using a pocket dictionary, she translated enough of the application to fill in her name, address and phone number. As she walked back to the apartment with groceries and her first supermarket card in hand, she couldn’t help but notice everyone had cell phones no matter how poor they were.

Young people dressed like rappers in designer clothes. How could they manage it? Imports would cost a fortune and the country didn't use the euro so their currency was worth less, so much less. As much as she hated cities, these new surroundings were making her homesick for Manhattan, like it was the place to be for a stroll in the country. Would it feel as crowded as it used to? The thing is, she'd never lived in Manhattan; been to Radio City for the Christmas show and to Rockefeller Center for the tree and angels. Don't forget Sabrett and hot pretzels from the vendors. She let the memory wrap its arms around her.

***Presage***

Available: practiced, experienced, knowledgeable, personable
Could only be an asset
But what is this I find
What I did years ago I am now overqualified for
And not beneficial
How can that be

There are too many students useful for programming
To be pushed around and paid less
Not fair to them or me
Still, I'm not asking for gold bars
Gee
I am not hired for positions needing no prior experience
Not confused but wondering
I'd be the ace up your sleeve

But I am educated, BAs and MAs
How many do you wish
Have taught in foreign countries
Internationally savvy, desired in these times
Am certified to teach
How is it
My peers hold MAs and are hired as teachers
I am required to seek more education
Why is it

My certification is wrong because it is overseas
I am a qualified professional yet not qualified enough
I am undependable because I am traveled
Why not resilient, flexible, a durable asset
I am accomplished but there needs be more
How much more though more is fine with me
But more deters your favor, your choice
Too much is your reply

Those who demand more education, more expertise
and "then of course..."
Don't have in the small print they will buy
Why not support
The burden forever my
Over and over in renewed surprise

I never expected all doors to be closed.
Stunned, but no one tells why
Don't blame the Economy
Let it languish in peace
Business Generalizations 101
Convenience in a whitewash lie

***That's Life***

All was quiet for a while after I got home; I wasn't locked out. One of the girls from the main floor came downstairs and said hello. I looked up and said "ah, one of the people who hates me". She said she didn't hate me and we talked a moment. A little later I was in the kitchen cooking soup, cream of mushroom with broccoli, and sautéing fresh tuna - so you know from that my fridge hadn't been ransacked as payback and my food survived - when one of the guys came down and gave me a hug. He said, "I can think for myself and make my own decisions. I don't hate you."

Afterward, I'd gone upstairs to check the recycle in the main-floor kitchen and see if any other bags needed to be put out. Needless to say C.J. came down from the top floor, walked past me and just like the officer predicted, she started in again. This time I wouldn't talk to her, no matter what I'd say it would spark an argument so I had nothing to lose, and she flew off the handle yelling so everyone could hear and threatened to start a petition against me; I've hit the big time - boycott Maggie! “You’re a horrible person! Horrible! I’m going to tell everyone to sign a paper and have Joe throw you out of the house!” I guess that’s one way to boycott a person! I wondered if I were helping by thinking it at all, adding positive karma to the success of her quest… huh, well… the thought'd slipped out, it’s too late now. I went back downstairs and could overhear her attempt to rally the household against me. Don't ask why but I climbed the stairs again, I knew there were at least two people not biting at the suggestion anyway, and stood behind her as she ranted on. At this point I had nothing to lose; I kept silent and listened. When she finished her tirade she went back to her room and I to mine. Later on she slid a typed note under my door that was a series of sentences ultimately putting all the blame on me. I used to help students like her when I was a conversation partner volunteer for the intensive English program on campus. I gave it the speed-skim once-over, did my best to keep my teacher brain in check and filed it. “Don’t file it”, my friend emailed back. “Make a copy and show the police. They want to know anyway.” “That’s easy enough”, I typed back. “A new week, a new circular file. I can retrieve it.”

I didn’t see anyone the next day with so many errands to run, and several little jobs to get accomplished. When I’d gotten back, the girl who didn’t hate me was cooking in the kitchen. “Thanks for the note”, she said sadly. “I just wanted you to know”, I said as I was passing, “that I understand if you want to move but you’re one of the good things in this house, one of the good people.” I smiled just slightly still feeling a bit of yesterday’s gut-wrenching heaviness no one but me knew I felt inside, and headed down the stairs. She had a pained look on her face; I think she would’ve given me a hug if I’d paused a little longer. Not having my heart in it at all, I dove into my studies and prepared lessons for students I’d be tutoring in a few hours. I felt a freedom when it was close to the time to go. I don’t usually get to leave from the house and tutor; I leave from my daylong volunteering and have a ton of stuff to cart with me so this was a treat. I took a tote bag and put the hour's lessons in it, then positioned it over my shoulder; I was traveling light! I sensed positive anticipation as I drove and I embraced it. The lesson went well even with the added resistance from the boy of the house, my older student, middle school age. He never wants more school after school, so he fell into his "I no speak English" mode. It wasn't the first time so I worked my usual magic and turned things into a good lesson in spite of what I'd been noticing as his steadily conforming westernization. How easily the children want to be just like Americans and kick tradition to the curb; my how they grow so quickly! His sister was in the mood to excel, polishing off worksheet after worksheet. When it was over both kids bolted downstairs like they always did. As I was still packing I heard them arguing, speaking at a pace that was like machine gun fire in their high-pitched foreign language; the one I was looking forward getting to know but didn't know yet. I dealt with Turkish for the two years I'd lived in Istanbul, I could face another non-Latin based language; let me at it! With their raised voices there was a certain amount of whining, and lord knows what else; I didn't hear anything breaking. I chuckled to myself, "families are the same the world over."

I entered the foyer to sit in the chair specially decorated by the daughter, grammar school age, for me, pull my boots on, get my tiny check and noticed as dad was carrying on with his usual banter his English wasn't so good either; in fact, now that I thought about it, it'd stopped being good the last lesson I was there. I hadn't put any importance on the change and had chalked it up to exhaustion; he's studying to be an economist. Being in the midst of studying for an MBA, I'd taken an Economics class – very involved stuff; I could relate. "Maggie, I have something I must tell you..." his voice shook and he looked ashamed. I received my pay and a pink slip. For the first time in a long while the entire family walked me out to my car. I'd never considered when they all didn't accompany me they were demonstrating disrespect and disapproval (now we get traditional); dad wanted me there but the rest of the family didn't. Mom and the kids had big smiles as they said goodbye. "Oh my goodness", I pulled over after I went around the corner out of sight to check where I'd put the check; this wouldn't be the best time to misplace it.

I thought of the gift my son was giving me so I could buy something special, and how I'd spent a small amount of it, by using other money I'd budgeted knowing I could replace it, on a piece of expensive fish. I momentarily wished I hadn't but it was too late for that, my tuna had been delicious and there was even some left over I was looking forward to having another day. My mind whirred figures and what resources: odds and ends, DVDs, jewelry, I had left to sell. When I got home, I watched a movie. I couldn't handle anything more right then; I had to let the past couple of days take their place. The movie I'd rented through my digital video library was terrible; I guess it would follow that it should have been. I got into my studies afterward and put together an assignment that would only need a facelift: an "I" or two dotted, the punctuation checked, when I'd give it the once over the next morning. The day had been productive in spite of it all.

I spoke with one of the other teachers from the same group who was also tutoring foreign students about a week later. Apparently, all the families let those of us in that small group go. Why? Who knows. They all lived in the same development and had gone on a vacation to Disney World together. A clue or not, it didn't make me feel much better or help, but I appreciated knowing I wasn't alone.

***Italian Alps***

Wandering through town
Bitter cold winter clouds
Drifted low today
Uninvited settled, wrapping embrace
Amazing, perfect, chilling the bone
Facial purifying features taut toned
As the streets filled with mist
Lest we look down
Glance over mountain's crown
Of gods get a glimpse

***Cazzarola***

Italian men sit wine in hand

At a table next to me in the café
Wish I spoke Italian better
What can I say?
Together we watch football
The European way
A gentler sport I've not seen
With a team of great gams
I can watch it
All day

I sip my Prosecco
Enjoy the platter
Cheeses and meats
Safe to walk the streets
Until it ends I'll stay
The darkness so peaceful
Many stars shine so bright
Nowhere in the world have I seen them
Casting off such a light
I wrap my arm around the night
Together we stroll away

The next day cappuccio
A balcony overlooks what's beneath
Then a walk to a Saint's house
Balanced on a pinnacle
Name all the mountains so high
They surround me, air so crisp
I'm held steady in the arms of the sky
The roads wind back
I walk while clouds happen by
Filling the streets with eerie mist
Such scenery
I'd never want to miss
I can get used to this

Maybe down to the market
For food so fresh
A bottle of wine, maybe two

Prosecco of my own
Or pizza at the pub
More football to see
What's the time, I don't know
Not a care to me
Monday rolls around, there'll be work to do
Cappuccio served with brioche
Life is important
And just for you

At day's end back to the mountains
Back to the café
Or maybe the pub this time
Is it closed?
Taken off from the week
Doesn't matter
Pour my whiskey drink
Tonight I'll write
Lively, noisy little place
People walk by, some come in
Later on, I sit back
Tomorrow more work
My head on night's shoulder
We stroll, together again

***An American Muse***

While strolling through Nişantaşı on a July 5th:

Yesterday was the 4th, yay America, but let us reflect on freedom from what; British tea, which has grown in popularity over the years, no kings, ok, but plenty of queens and Moet de Chandon, pretty cabinets notwithstanding.

***Resurrection Day***

It's sad I guess, no one wanted to talk
All too busy with each other
Lack of truths hurts the heart

Even expected, heaviness weighs
But it's resurrection day

To commemorate what
Brutality, murder, abandonment
How could you leave me this way?
But wait, that was past Friday
Why hear it today?

So I'm sitting here now
Heavy-hearted anyway
How soon before I'm told
Don't bother anymore
Life with you is just too old

There're others now
No history they hold
Easier to deny, easier to unfold
You never happened here
No memory to hold dear

No turning back from this
A forward path anew
New life forever clear
Never liked you anyway
Makes it easier to do

A culture steeped in sin
The deadliest and true
Look away, turn around
Remove the stars, the bars
Not worthy of our ranks
We're finished now with you
Neatly placed right in the trash
Be free to be all that you are
It will not touch us, it's all your scar
Laugh head thrown back, safe from afar

# *Stories And Storms*

***Not A Nor' Easter But A Mid' Wester***

Two days of 73 yet New York's buried in snow
Trees down electric out
I want to be cozy in winter clothes
Hot cocoa, peppermint, electric fireplace glow
Tired of muggy warm with November
An appointment the 3rd wouldn't you know
50 and rainy slight whipping around
Getting there I suppose, winter could get closer
Walking's good cardio I have this umbrella
The size 3 friends fit beneath
It could work, that I'm pleased
I'll enjoy being dry, no more compacts for me

Made my destination
Now to walk home in more rain
Wind picked up I wonder
Could I fly, let it lift me
No, I might lose control, should I diet, would it help
Thoughts interrupted, umbrella sucker punch in a gust
I dodge and a miss
Turn turn again not letting it bend back
We wrestle another gust
Turn left turn right I am victorious
Cars driving by no wipers on I see
Close the umbrella winds keep stray drops away
Blow past not given time to alight, slight tingle on my face
The rain won't agree comes down just enough
Face the wind, open again, a man passes scowled look
Almost impaled as I re-engaged
Oops
Tilt up down peek around I struggle through campus
Everyone else is safe

All directions gust, make my way into town
I twist I turn I turn again almost lifted
No cars, light's red, umbrella tugs my hand
Twist, leaning, shawl blows across off a shoulder

Flies front, strap holds, one block more ahead
Sudden lull, rest, a camisole in the sun
Gust, turn around brace again
Hurry up stairs to a covered front porch
Close umbrella glance back at the labyrinth behind
Inside clothes dry, droplets shake off
Shoes soaked up the sidewalks, ah, for others dry feet
You're welcome
My thoughts on a sardonic note
Go out for galoshes later, designer
A lining that's warm
This time I'll drive, enough braving the storm

### *At The "Tav"*

It was a Sunday afternoon and
Even after watching a splendid variety of vampire drama
I know I'm not compelled in what I say
I'd made such a healthy Sunday dinner and thought I'd find dessert
Setting out reliving in my mind the poor selection I know I'll find
According to my taste buds anyway
How the Cafés have no variety and limited cakes in my Midwestern exile, I'm from the east you see
Intriguing were desserts in Istanbul, a place that redefined sweets for me
A more unique variety in Middle Eastern cuisine
Deciding a place to go I mused, "what are the odds" then journeyed back
We used to meet up the three of us and all the friends
Those regulars who lent character and helped create atmosphere
You cooked so your sister'd be spoiled but you're not there now
It caught in my throat, as I walked not far from my place
What kind of exercise can I call that
But how will it feel, a question I didn't have to ask

So I thought about the desserts I might find, noticing my reflection as

I passed restaurant glass, a little jab to distract from the stab
Well I talked myself out of Death by Chocolate right then
Not in shape for that yet, does that make sense
I read through the menu, crossed decadence off my list to settle for
A scoop with chocolate sauce and iced coffee
The place never made espresso no sense to complain and it was
All that my pocketbook would allow anyway so
I combined them both into Coffee Royal as the cicadas
drowned music piped out to the patio
Yes cicadas decided to stop by and start the summer off
Numerous as any biblical plagues eating trees in their path
The coffee should mellow the white wine and liquor I had
earlier
So I can walk and smooth out what I saw in my reflection
and aid digestion
But when all's said and done, I don't think I'll go there
anymore
Miss you son

### *Thor Could Be a Really Fun Boyfriend*

She closed the book, placed it on the table and finally decided to walk through the door. Forgetting there was no back deck because of remodeling, she absent-mindedly unlocked the door and stepped through falling face first in the mud, managing to kiss the corner of a rock with the side of her head. She came-to with a gentle nudge... nudge... nudge, "hey… hey… hello there… hey". Leaning over her was a T-Rex with long arms; at least that's what she thought she saw. He smiled with a lot of teeth that were very white. "I'm your neighbor Cole. Are you ok?" "Huh?" Still a little too stunned by the fall to make a lot of sense she slurred, "You talk... y-yh-hhh… yhoo tahl... k." Her eyes rolled back, her body went completely limp. She dreamt of falling in and into darkness, as if an uncomfortable slumber were taking hold. Her body jerked suddenly, she opened her eyes with a start and after a few moments became aware she was on the ground staring up at a t-shirt from the local paleontology museum with a smiling Tyrannosaurus screen printed on the chest, made that way for the sake of children paying a visit to the exhibit.

The long, very well toned arms she'd seen were attached to something else, or rather, someone else. Raising her eyes, her stupor began to clear with the realization they belonged to her neighbor, the very man she'd arranged her lunch schedule around to watch work out in the company gym through the picture window facing her office. Adolescent glee shot through every crevice of her body as she instantly, silently ordained it might just take her a while to get back on her feet; in fact, how long could be negotiable or better yet, it wouldn't be. "Could life get much better than this?" sent a thrill through every single facet of her being as he offered to help her get cleaned up and take her to the E.R. if she needed it. He wrapped her arm around his neck as he put his around her back, lifting her up for support, which couldn't stop her knees from buckling not so much from the fall but from the sheer pleasure of his touch, his smell, being glued against the side of his body, his *everything*. He didn't stumble as she shakily hobbled around her house to the front door, which luckily had been left unlocked. "Look, I hope you don't mind, but…" and he gallantly swept her into his arms carrying her through the front door. Her inner Psyche smiled large as she thought, "Now it's going to get good."

***Not So Surreal: A Very Short Story***

Nela sat curled up listening to the conversations of the humans surrounding her concerning her needs, what she liked, should have and didn't mind. As if! Twelve pounds of fury and she knew being a Rat Terrier, her purpose was chasing Rats. "And they didn't even euthanize me, what's it called - being 'put to sleep'- like I'd be waking from that, after I snapped at the baby" ran through her mind. "I thought that'd be offense enough for some kind of action. At least then I'd be in heaven (yes, we go to heaven too) looping around cloudy fields chasing more rodents than I could count, (what would they say if they knew I could count - hah!) but instead, I'm living in apartments with no yards being walked on a leash twice a day as if bodily functions worked on cue. If they'd at least give me away I'd have a chance winding up at a home that had a yard; then I'd be able to have a little fun... Oh, no; the baby's awake!" She jumped off the couch and darted toward the kennel on the far side of the dining room table. "Whew... made it!."

## *Arguing With The Buttons Of My Jacket: An Ode To Transvestites*

There were a pronounced number of transvestites in Madrid and those numbers would increase the closer I got to Sol, Madrid's town center, which was also an extraordinarily popular-always crowded tourist attraction. I'd pass many on the streets as I walked around and many of them became familiar faces. Some managed heels better than others; one in particular wore the coolest belly rings:

*Transvestite*

Transvestido
Transvestite Castellano
Transdress
Hombre-Mujero
Otre Gazpacho
Caliente no frio
Gaucho gazpacho, South Americans in Spain
But they can't walk in heels
Not well but don't complain
The transvestidos not South Americanos
Heelo cambinaro like chago or was it chango
Camminaro-transvesto
Adam's Apple no discreto
Discreeto
No way-o, that's via
O vio gay calle
That's streeto, Gay Street
No habla Españolo
Too early to tell-o
That's hablo pozuelo
A place-o to go-o
El barrio for bagel-o
El barrio quatro
El barrio para
Pero paro trans-tido.

***52º Ode***

The clocks moved forward saving daylight once again
Thank-goodness for that
But I went walking this morning an hour later than I should
It felt good
Tomorrow I will walk in dark light, greet the day later on
And will always bring my mace
That I walk in peace, be warned
Know your place
And there be no pain in another face
But the snow is melting thank you fifty-two degrees
Curbside rivers running
I have sidewalks again
I stomped snow into streams
Watching ice float away as I played
My choice to walk the peaceful street or not
Even at that time of day all stay in bed, hide
Time to get up, what, what, no way!
No worries of cars on ice or
Lightening fast will I get away?
Only of the all night stoner who
Shouldn't be on the road at night
Never mind the day
Or the all-night worker
Finding his, or is it her morning way
Or the drunk always drunk
A legal habit with a price all pay
But spring is coming, and winter begone
I enjoyed my walk with promising spring sun

But the next day winter had something to say

Winter strikes back at spring
Windy mist sting with
Glassy ice splinters unseen
Passing a streetlight
They gust by uncloaked

In rainy spray frozen
Under a morning night sky
Sharp pinch on my lashes
Flutter over my eye
But winter won't win this argument
I know
Soon enough it will have to go

***Discrimination Made Simple***

*Most definitely a storm, this is the original piece "Presage" from the title STAGES is based on*

What I did years ago I am now found overqualified for

There are too many students useful for programming
To be pushed around and paid less
I am not hired for positions needing no prior experience

I am an educated woman, two BAs, two MAs
Have taught in foreign countries
Am certified to teach
And although my peers hold MAs only and are hired as teachers
I am required to seek more education
My certification is wrong because it is overseas
I am a qualified professional not qualified enough
I am undependable because I am traveled
I am accomplished but it's not good enough
Those who demand more education, more expertise and then of course...
Don't have in the small print that they will buy

The burden always my

***Spring***

The bear wandered closer to get a good look
A young kid, next companion for lunch

I'll get cool and calm
He won't know a thing
I'll come back here later
We'll munch

***Excelsior***

*It was late October of 2002*

*I was subbing in New York at a local school district and 9/11 was still too new. The children of a 5th grade class I was permanently assigned to had a project to do with designing Utopia, concocted by their teachers and their Guidance Counselors, in hopes of bringing out how they felt inside about all that'd happened. I was touched and inspired by these kids in their candor and simplicity of their solution, in the way they collaborated and shared their ideas that became one universal design.*

Olim paulitas
Capio Ulyssius
Iter facio sinistra
Videre quis non et
Nova vita forte esse

Once upon a time with children yet so small
I took Ulysses journey across a land west
To see what we could see that new life perhaps could be

Years later and more grown yet feeling still alone
Small children now no longer
Ulysses, journey back with me
Is this place still my home, let's see
Excelsior! The place doth cry and I muse
What do they say?
I must think perhaps must analyze a state in such a way
My Latin book I opened wide
Intellectual heights will rise
Wisdom will pass the sky (way high)
My mind takes off to fly
"Out of or down from high" I read, I think

'From haughtiness, nay, that I might reach the sky'
I read once more, a deponent verb, a passive form in active meaning
More than meets the eye

"Something happening to me now in being that I am
Present, passive, indicative, I am becoming
I am, I will be"
All so complex

Then the kids of my 5th grade class taught all this to me
As I was subbing one fateful day
What excelsior is and forever will be
Was set forth from the mouth of babes:

Out of the ashes we will rise, we will be once more
We have no need to settle in violence a new score
Utopia we design this time with outer chutes and slides
That fun and safety reign and happiness attain
Until your soul is purified from fire and from flame you caused
Until the world is one and no more of this pain
Forth from this confinement the ash can harden not nor separate
That united we will stay

# A Way Tall Tale

***Jack The Ribbett***

Hideous, Horrible, Horrendous the Beast
Wandered downtown hungry for a human feast
Picking his teeth with leftover big toe
What was he exactly, could he be a big troll
Honestly now I can't say yes or no but
Where he's just come from we never will know

He walked into an Inn and exclaimed in a roar
"Rounds are on me" but they ran out the door
The barkeep confused said, "How's one on the house!"
Jack reached out and grabbed him, ear to ear grinned his mouth
"Now that sounds just fine, you'll be good enough"
As he twisted and turned him wrung him into a cup
Then he tossed what was left toward a far corner right there
And grabbed for the blender, then sat down in a chair

"Now I'll make a thick milkshake", Ribbett growled a gulp
"A milkshake for me made of field mice and spiders
The tarantula's size is such a juicier kind,
I'd like those the best, and I need a mouse's nest
First he shook crystal web made of tatter and shimmer
The spider peeked out just too late
He was dinner
A field mouse ran by and was stomped underneath
By Jack's old leather boot
Now he's ridges and streaks
Jack just dusted him off put him in the blender's jar
Added barkeep blood and spider pressing frappe so far

He sat feet perched up as his drink swirled and curled
And he thought it'd be nice if he had a sweet girl for his dinner to eat
That would be quite a treat
Well, wouldn't you know
Just then came a child who was twelve or thirteen
And for all of her life knew just how to be mean
She was mean to the postman, she was mean to the cat

She was mean to her mother now imagine just that!
She was mean to all bugs and especially crickets
She was mean to snakes too
Wrapped them up in thick thickets at the end of thick sticks
Looking so much like wicks
Then lighting them up so that torches they play
When she walked from school late snakes lit up all the way
Just perfect was she for beast feasting this day
She walked passed the Inn and she saw Jack the Ribbett
But before she could say
Any mean words on her mind toward his way
His long tongue shot out snatched her up in a flick
And he swallowed her whole
Switched off frappe one click
Drank down his thick mixture from the blending big cup
He threw his head back belched out loud his last gulp
Jack reached into his pocket
He reached way down deep
Threw two bits on the barkeep may he rest now one piece
For the ferryman's fee, the change he could keep
Then he walked toward the doorway and gave back one last glance
"Nice place, cozy town
I'll stop here again when I get back from France."

### *Jack The Ribbett Almost Makes It To France*

Still Hideous, Horrible, Horrendous that Beast
On his way to France had an Italian feast
He looked at the map bit the toe and the heel
And thought to himself, "that's not good for a meal
I'll stop off at Italy, well known for cuisine to
Make my mark known on the local food scene"
He looked at the map again, thought "well I am here"
As he traced with beast finger to It'ly right there
"I must get to the ocean and swim from that beach
It shouldn't take too long, three days to two weeks"

He swam from New England, from Maine's rocky coast

To the shores of Italia, the ones near to Rome
He stood on the sand, shook himself off from his swim
And he looked around wondering just where to begin
He still wasn't hungry filled with mean girl and frappé
"I'll start walking a while toward the mountains going that way
I'll be good for my health" he thought to himself
He walked and he walked, then he climbed and
Climbed more, he didn't get lost
Up ahead was a town surrounded by walls
And he thought it a good place he'd stop at and call
But for people who lived there what would be the cost
So he went into that town that was there in the north
And he looked people over
"What'd be good for a broth" he said right out loud
"I'll add onions and pepper and garlic so white
With mushrooms and tomatoes to simmer all night"
But when Jack looked around, no one took to flight

He saw women with aprons and a man with a hat
There were children with gelato
Gelato, what's that!
Someone came with three pizzas
And said, "try these instead
One has olives, one has sausage, and one five kinds of cheese
Much better than people and so tasty if you please

Now try some dessert made from pigs' feet and knuckles
We'll get that broth started to drink on the side
All the food we are making we make with great pride
It's an act we enjoy, mange, mange we say"
Jack the Ribbett sat down
He'd been walking all day

He thought "better than people, now how can that be
Better than spiders, better than mean girls
I'll just have to see"
He ate twenty pizzas while the broth simmered slow
He ate some dessert and then it was done

So he drank down the broth, tasted good
This was fun

He asked for a big toe to pick his teeth clean
But the man in the hat gave him twigs from a stream
That was rolling ever calmly by the outskirts of town
"If you're done", he said gently "feel free to leave now
We've made you a raft while you enjoyed your great feast
To help you to France, it'll take just one week
If you leave with the current and the way it is flowing"
Jack grinned ear-to-ear "well I'd better get going"

So the people escorted Hideous-Horrible to the bank
And handed him a thermos with a grocery sack
"Now take these things with you to enjoy your long trip
Say hello to the people in France"
They all waved as he sailed out to sea
Jack sat there full belly in a trance
"He doesn't know what happened", said the man with the hat
"Just the way it should be… hee… hee... hee... hee... hee..."

As Jack floated away he slowly thought to himself
"Hey I had no Italians to eat
In fact all I had was pigs' knuckles and feet
I wonder if French people'd be good for that
Spicy or bitter would they make a good broth
Or a soup stock with onions, that's it
How many would I use for hearty French onion soup
How many are good in a dip?"

***Jacques Le Ribbette***

What would he do if he made it to France
The beast thought as he sailed on still somewhat confused
"I can't believe it, I ate not one Italian", he continued in his state of bemused
"I want French Onion Soup made of Frenchmen of course"
As the raft bumped the shore of a smaller stream beach

And Jack wondered if he'd sailed the right way
He decided to get out and just look around
If but only for one half a day

He stood and he stretched looking this way and that
Wouldn't you know there was another man wearing a hat
Standing under a sign that read "oooh, la, la, la
Welcome to France's smaller stream beach number nine
"That's better" thought Jack "and he looks tasty too"
As he asked him "is downtown this way?"
"Ouiiiiiii…" the man replied as he slid down Jack's throat
"This is the best I've felt since my past Italian stay"

As Jack walked downtown women shrieked and they ran
"Well this certainly wasn't a part of my overall plan"
So he stood by a man and he hid Ribbett tongue
"What's your name" the man asked and the Ribbett replied
"Jacques le Ribbette" was the last thing he said
As his mouth closed real tight right over the man's head
Someone standing real close overheard every word

Before Jack turned around
Someone'd run into the square
"Jacques le Ribbette, Jacques le Ribbette
Beware, all beware!"
The street cleared before him
They closed all French shops
They pulled down their French shades
And locked all French locks
Right before Jack's eyes, it was such a surprise

Jack's mood got real glum and he just
Pouted a pout "well at least I had a couple Frenchmen
Before this came about
I'll go back to the raft at stream beach number nine
What will I do, now I have so much time
I guess I'll sail on down to England or Spain
I'll sail far into the sea and I'll sail in the rain!"

He found his way through to the raft and was caught
By the sun that was setting so bright
He stood there and watched, his back to the land
Ignoring the French dead silent sound
No one's coming out till he wasn't around
On that one they're standing their ground
Then he left as day turned into the night

"I'll sail on right now" he thought to himself
"I'm tired and full enough so I'll sleep
Maybe I'll wake again this same time next week"
So Jack fell asleep to the sway of the tide
The best of the dreams all filling his mind
At least twelve tasty mean girls with
Mugs full to the rim of thick spider frappe
And a pile of Frenchmen, to snack on the side
So much decadence his favorite sin
He dreamt on, his mouth in a grin that kept spreading ever so wide
Grunt-grunting, snort-snorting Jack rolled to his side

### ***Snake In A Lawn Chair Tanning In The Sun***

*Have You Ever Seen This One? But, it really happened on a day in the sun.*

A perfect sultry day
For a sultry woman
In her sultry way

Two chairs in the yard
"On this one I'll stay"
Laying oils and a book underneath
Eyes closed as she breathed summer heat

He fell from above her dangling low from the tree
Curled right up and erect in a hiss
She opened her eyes and said, "What is this
This is no way to lay in the sun and you're ruining my tan number one!"

So she took him and stretched him right by her full length in the chair that was there by her side
He was a curious looking creature with thick full snake lips and the widest expressive snake eyes

Then she reached underneath for her oils and such and she rubbed his full length the way down
As his snake frown quick turned upside down
And his snake tongue twitched round and around
Then the two of them lay and soaked up the sun as their skin just turned browner and brown

She turned to him then and to her so surprised his eyes were shut closed with his skin crinkle dried and the biggest of grins grinning wide
And she leaned and she whispered with the gentlest breath “time to turn now and even things up” as his skin started crumbling to dust

So she blew on the dust, he disappeared in a puff
Swirling and tossed with the wind
Followed by that biggest of grins that got wider the higher he flew
She would never have thought she could blow him away
Who knew it could ever be true!
She just lay so surprised as she watched his grin rise getting wider and wider as it tumbled and tossed
And she couldn’t help thinking “well just look at you” the higher and higher he flew.

# Where Do You Think You Get It From

***Some Things You'll Never Be Old Enough To Know***

Did I ever awaken still in a post wastenotic state, (who'd ever heard of vodka and gatorade anyway) too incoherent to remember where his living room light switch was, where I had dropped my clothes, why I'd dropped them; if there were a lamp on the end table by the couch I could turn on?

In the complete darkness I put my hand on the arm of the sofa he had passed out on, later on I could reflect on why I was on the floor, directly onto my keys and knew which one was to my home where my children and his slept. I grasped those keys and held out the one to unlock my door. I felt my way to his kitchen, put one hand flat on the door, with the other leaned elbow to wrist to steady myself in an attempt to focus by looking through the peephole. Cracking the door open, I peeked outside onto a perfect, clear frozen night. In the full moon the darkness was still, breezeless, densely cold below zero, and for February rightly so. The snow and trees shimmered in ice. I stood barefoot, clutched the key tight with stirring resolve, threw open the door and began to run letting it slam behind me. I knew he would not wake. As it click-locked I began to pray to a god in whom I did not believe that I would not drop my keys and be caught freezing, shivering, naked.

(Couldn't remember where my clothes were, remember? Neither did I.)

Internally tensing as a commander demanding a salute, I pushed any physical sensing outside of me forbidding my body to feel the cold. I ran up three steps to my door; the key entered the lock perfectly. I pulled it open hurrying inside sliding under blankets covering huddled children on my living room floor. The door slammed locked behind me waking no one. In the coziness I began violent trembling from the cold, then slowly became relaxed in creeping warmth beginning from my toes. I fell into a slumber knowing I should dress before the children woke. A few hours later I rose; the sunrise was perfect, brilliant and the day densely cold.

Mother, did you ever do anything like we might do? (Not that we'd do anything like that!) Would you ever dance naked in the moonlight? Of course not and I would never would be the gentle reply, but I upped them one and that I will forever deny.

***I Could Be Ageless***

When I knew I was older with each coming year,
Maturity way beyond my time
I was fiery enough to stand up and defy
Someone acting appalled concerning my mini
Made from the finest wool I would buy.

At least two feet of fabric to cover, there were
That could no way keep unfrozen my thighs,
Covered with tights, thicker hose not warm enough
Turning deep red I waited, I waited for the bus
As so many cars drove by.

I remember that biker who punctually rode past
Every season always high on the ride;
A smile and face glowing, it struck me
So cool
And I knew he was my kind of guy.

Now I know, never doubt
How to be young, to be vibrant,
There's wisdom enough left
Save the spittle I guess
Serves no need for another one’s eye.

I can stay seated, be relaxed
Or just walk along calm,
I know who I am, with that is no qualm
Cantankerous, could be brilliant,
Had you asked me I'd tell you that’s why
My reflection in a soft drawn-out sigh

### *Advice For Any Apocalypse*

My friend and I would visit each other regularly. My 4-year old son would walk with me to her house and play with her 5-year old while she and I shared a bottle of Soave and discussed life in general. Her then fiancée's parents were members of a faith that had the inside scoop about the end of the world. They were so certain their members, including themselves, were selling all worldly possessions and gathering at the meeting place to be taken up; they knew the day, the place and the hour. His parents kept calling him, warning him to be prepared.

Toward the end of our conversation, I asked my friend if she thought the world might really end. Reflecting for less than a second she said, "There's no sense worrying if it is." "True, that's true. I'll see you tomorrow unless the world ends. Maybe we'll be meeting somewhere that never runs out of Soave."

I awoke the next morning to a gorgeous Indian-Summer day; in New York and New England the autumn is always dramatically brilliant. My son and I kicked up leaves as we walked. My friend's front door was open welcoming the unseasonably warm; she already had the Soave ready. "Well, the world didn't end." "No, it didn't. What about your fiancée's folks? Did they get rid of *everything*...?"

### *An Italian-American Studying Spanish In Spain*

A bit of perverse verse that followed a language lesson for me. I was the student at large with my passion for learning set free. As you read consider it's you on my brain like those inane adverts comparing fried eggs to drugs. Are they the ones insane, is it just me, possibly all of us? Together we'd make a fine bowl of nuts.

*Syllogismo Hypothetico 101*

Or hypothetical syllogism on a
Developing Spanish brain
Habla No Español
Could be a crying shame

After all is said and done
This is what I have to say

Poco Loco
No muy pero
Mucho Loco
Cocoa Loco
Coco Loco
Coco Richo Bicho
No poco dinero
Muy Mucho
Loco mucho dinero
Wanto be richo
Richo like bicho
No bicho es bug-o
Bicho es richo con mucho dinero
Mi scrive con headacho
Es scrive 'Taliano
Pero mi Italiana
Scribo escriva
Who cares!
Con huevo
Con hueso
An egg or a wrist
Make my food by hand?
If you insist!

Para aqui? Si si!
Aqui para me
No mi pero me
Poro mi? See, see!
No sea, no see
Pero si, si, si, si!
Starbucks espresso con tearos
Tearos no 'spañol
Españolo para tearo?
No tiendo!
No tieno?

I don't knowlo
Understando oro havo
Oro goldo
No goldo!
Oro tieno.

Hasta luego
Luego see you latero
Latero lateral
Lateral no Españo
Lateral es linea
Linea es tren
Linea es meho
Meho es pano
Español es ce (they)
They uno
They dos
Dos progama o programo uno eme
Emmy is nombre
Nombre es name-o
No number is numero
So?

Medicino assistencia
Para Headacho
Headacho Españo
Braino paino
Oh... oh...
I don’t know.
Fell lightheaded, no feel lightheaded es
Illuminato
Illuminato Italiano?
Illuminato Demolitionato Mano?
Illuminata Italiana, so vero.
Si vero, Italiana Españana, Españata?
Posiblo? No, posibla!
Finito Syllogismo-o-a
Si, si here it goes.

Aqui es so, boy, yo?
Habla Español?
:. No

***Be Resilient, Try Things, Check The World Out***

I flew in to New York and took an endless shower in Manhattan, the land of hot water that never runs out, or so it seemed to me. Before we went to the apartment, I bought my face cream at a 24-hour drug store that I might indulge in the fountain of youth for $5.95; abroad I have to travel with enough jars or else I'm lost; they don't sell what I want most places; besides, I haven't found a 24-hr drugstore yet. I didn't mind I was paying 2 dollars more than what I usually pay outside the city; it was just great to be back. I rose at 4:15 but from where I had been that is 11:15 A.M. so I've slept late; 4th dimensionally speaking, I hadn't slept that late since I was a teenager. My little brother sleeps, yes he has a flat downtown, wait, mind lapse, I'm in the States; remember to say apartment. He's not so little anymore in his early 40s, but I'm still the oldest; he hasn't caught up yet. It's dark on 21st street and the city is at peace, an ambience of quiet for a city that never sleeps:

One of my students had asked me, "How can that be, people in New York are awake 24-hours a day with no rest? If the city never sleeps then no one sleeps. People have to sleep." She said it almost angrily as if that's a desired trait and why can't she do it! No one else in the class had any ideas on it (according to Berlitz they were second level - beginners first class); a lesson in defining "what's a shift" and idiomatic expression, "the city never sleeps" was due and happened next. I assured her and the rest of the class people sleep the same as they do; like a hospital, if an establishment stays open all night, different people work there different times of the day to keep it open, so in a nutshell, (oops, there's another idiom) a city, any city that boasts it's a city that "never sleeps" means if you can't sleep there's always something to do to pass the time; many places stay open 24/7, 24 hours a day for 7 days a week. We didn't get into cab availability or bus and subway schedules, or into the fact that if you are there between 4 and 6 A.M., most likely there'll be maintenance going on. After all, the place needs to be cleaned and kept up. I realized New York City has quite a reputation! It's a supernatural place of wonderment.

"When wonderment awakes it won't be heard here just a couple of blocks from the noise, interesting how that works in a location just close enough to get involved and just far enough away to be out of the bustle", wrapped up my thought as I propped myself up and looked out the window. "So peaceful, good to be back... oh-no where did that truck come from? Ha, interrupting my meditation", but it's quiet again and soon we'll grab a coffee and such, then a cab to the airport and I'll travel on to where I will live for a while and begin life once again, this time from the States where everyone speaks English - not really. The thing here is students are thrown together as a U.N. - like it or not - classroom, as opposed to a classroom filled with students of one shared language, which makes for another type of innovative instruction and diplomacy. Welcome back!

***Advanced Turkish According To Me***

*Creating Universal Language*

*Borrowed from "An Elevator In Istanbul: No Elevator Yet, Take 2":*

I wasn't taking formal lessons but learning from living day-to-day attempting to communicate, and my brain being my brain, this is what came from doodling as fate had its way: An advanced Turkish lesson according to me. And the doodle goes on, just wait and see.

*Gardening In B-Town (Bakırköy that would B)*

"Bahçesi is garden of good vegetables for you
Bahçe is too, flower garden in bloom
Parchesi is thirsty or
Parçesi in Turkish (only a Turk would know)
Parcheesie a game
How do you spell parcheesey,
Parçeezi, par-cheesey

Not at all chessey
Good griefi, not griefee
Nor griefy no word
Oil on pizza pie to go

Pizzahçesi, pizza garden
Pizzahçesi, will it possibly sell
Pizza Bahçe, Pizzabahçe
The best marketing I'll insist
Or maybe Pizzabahcé with a French twist
Kahvebahçesi a coffee garden
Never heard of one of those
Subahçesi water garden or
Beach by Black Sea, by Marmara
The Bosphorus, a place of water falls
Currents collide, dolphins chatter with glee

Ekmekçesi, Ekbahçesimek
A bread garden of rolls
Ekmekbahçe
Kaiser, sub-sandwich
Lavaş or Pida
Lamacunbahçesi or
A garden of lamacun
Traditional baking you'll have to come try
The pizza of Turkey
Istanbulian cuisine
Istanbulbahçesi
A garden of people make a rolling
Sea wave of heads walking
In the square ahead of me
The road I can't now see
How is it we all fit
Just how can it be

Bar Bahçesi or Barçesi
Could we use a drink now
Paşabahçe is glassware
Ç – ch, ş – sh, ţ – th

Doesn't exist
Beţany, baţ, birţ, worţ
Nah, not used to this, but fun if it did
Merhababahçesi, too many syllables
Merhababa and her thieves
Make it his, blame to him
That sounds good to me
Merhabahçesi, a garden of hellos
Or a very big welcome
from mymerhaba.com

Goodbyebahçesi, not the yellow brick road
No gardens there that I know
Hoşça Kal Bahçesi, stay pleasantly garden
Or Garden of Eden
Utopia of sin when
Slithery and slimy neighbors move in
Utopiabahçe
Well, there went the hoodbahçesi, it's no more
Or the neighborhood garden, barriobahçesi
Does that invasion exist
Did those two worlds collide

But what I was thinking in Goodbye Bahçesi
A Bed and Breakfast as I'm just passing through
Hoşça Kal Bahçesi or Hoşça Kal Bahçe
That the sun always shine on you"

I think I could write greeting cards.

***Birthing***

An egg floated in a sea of salty tears. It hatched and Ra, the sun god, came forth from the River Nile, the source and sauce to spice life.

And Aphrodite rose, "I'm naked? I need clothes! There'd best be a Sachs, or there it's going to go! And, a place for a pedicure, just look at those toes!"

As Zero the Orbit watched from above, he called her Venus when she'd visit the stars. Although he was little, he was very hip with a spike at the top that reached to three planets. The comets traveling went up-down, up-down, up-down and back around, leaving a smooth trail.

Zeus looked up from many-ridged Olympus, the way he willed the great mount to be, pleased with the way the day had turned out. He boasted his power as over thrower of Titans but this was his best work by far.

***Arts***

Breathe in and hold it
Fingers snap, snap, snap, snap
Exhale and slow now
Clap, clap, clap, clap, clap
A room full of snakes as they slither away or
Balloons as the gas leaks
Hot air becomes grey

Hee, hee and hee, hee
Make it sharper you say
Ho, ho, ho, ho, ho as
The baritones sound
Ha, ha, ha, ha, ha
Become circus clowns

Now class pay attention
I want minds sharp as beaks
As we sing that new song we learned
All the last week
Let's stretch now and exhale
Do, mi, do, ti, re, ti

# *Stages II*

## *Priceless Perspectives*

*I was in the medical profession for ten years of my life, and my first position was as an aid at a Nursing Home. Some of my best and happiest memories were there. There is no pretense with the patients; they are who they are, honest, candid, and see things as they see them in spite of all that ails them, a priceless perspective it wouldn't hurt everyone to share.*

Will and Old Pete sat by the nurses' station looking out the window next to the emergency exit door discussing farm animals in the field. Some they knew by name and one had a calf not too long ago. "See that calf over there", Old Pete asked one of the nurses passing by. "A calf? Where is it?" "Over under those trees", he said. "That's a parking lot. There aren't any cows out there", she snapped in a stern voice and stomped on past. Will just looked at him and shook his head. Lillie had been passing by on the way to her room and overheard their conversation. She asked about the calf and how many cows were out there. She knew a little bit about farming herself.

A few minutes later I walked past her room and noticed Lillie was closing her curtains. It was still mid-afternoon and the sun was shining brilliantly. I asked why and she said, "You heard Pete and Will, didn't you? I don't want those cows looking in my window." I walked over to her window and looked outside. "You see cows too?" "Will and Pete do and they know about these things. I'm going to listen to them" "Sounds good", I quietly exhaled, "Lillie, you go right ahead if it makes you feel better", and I continued on making rounds.

## *Always Something To Be Learned*

Light is an intrusion on the peacefulness of the dark but I can't see to write otherwise my twisted thought provoking thought. The parting of the Red Sea is easily revealed; it was a major sandbar that everyone ran through except for the Egyptians. By the time they caught up the tide was coming in; wouldn't want to be them that day.

***Not A Word***

I have nothing to say
Can you believe it?
No way
I sit in the quiet surround
Ceiling fan spins round
And around

And around

And around

Press CTRL, ALT, DELETE
The screen says to me
I have no password you see
My speechless reply
Ceiling fan hums
Round and around

And around

And around

Voices next door
One sounds just
So bored
Second hand paces
3 seconds a beat
Time refuses to fleet

And round
And around

Don't mind the peace
One hour left or two
No more will do
Time better now fleet
I can go home

See my peeps

Not a bird that cheeps

And around

See my ceiling fan spin
Gently round and around
Let tomorrow begin
It'll get here soon
I relax in my room
Round and around

Breathing gentle soft sound

Ceiling fan, sleep

And around

***About Nieces***

It's too bad
Oh, So sad
Could've really been rad
Except for Dad
Won't always shell out the dough
Wouldn't you know
But she doesn't care
Like to live somewhere
Nearer to the sea
A southern place could be
And an accent sweet song
Might just help her along
Gut feeling to go
Running her own show
Where she is call home
A traveler will roam
Interesting places unknown
Don't give her any guff

She is woman
She is tough
No matter how old
Watch the plan unfold

***Mid Jet Stream***

*As winter battles spring for the right to stay, but it can't fight Punxsutawney Phil, the world's most accurate weatherman, and what he had to say:*

Adapted from: *52° Ode / Retaliate*
The snow is melting thank you fifty-two degrees
Curbside rivers running
I have sidewalks again
I stomped snow into streams
Watching ice float away as I played
My choice to walk the peaceful street or not
No worries of cars on ice or
Lightening fast will I get away?

*But the next day winter had something to say*

Winter strikes back at spring
Windy mist sting with
Glassy ice splinters unseen
Passing a streetlight
They gust by uncloaked
In rainy spray frozen
Under a morning night sky
Sharp pinch on my lashes
Flutter over my eye

***Architecture Worldwide And A Sphynx Aside***

Possibly holding the 8th, 9th, and 10th 'wonders of the world' spot for both ancient and modern times, the Kio Towers sit facing each other like Egyptian Sphinx or should it be Sphynx, heads tilted as if bowing in acknowledgement and respect of each other's grandness. They mark the entryway to the Centro, the business district of Madrid; their nod caught for eternity in acknowledgement, "Yes, you may pass." Made up of black glass and red windowpanes, each level section boasts four massive windows that house smaller, colonial panes for those corporations and companies that settle there. I'm told Caja Madrid owns them and rents - aquila - offers for acquisition, the office space inside.

The tower with the Caja Madrid logo on its side has a small fountain at it's front that waters useless, decorative rocks or although lifeless, are they an expression of Madridian business practice: tough, strong, dependable, agreeable and always listening with it's finger on the pulse? As I walked toward a front door believing the sharp-edged square construction, also claiming ground level made of tower girder material, may have been a seat that would have protected me from the evening winds in the buildings' lean-to embrace, I discovered it was a made-to-scale ashtray filled with sand. An opinion not etched in stone, but that's the first impression I had followed by an impulse I should just say no.

*A Sphinx aside fun part for speculation:*
Sphynx, spelled this way, is actually a hairless cat breed with its origination in North America, yet its noteworthiness is for the Egyptians. Sphinx, spelled this other way, is from Greek myth, known as the monster of Thebes and has a woman's head with a lion's body; the image with a human head is the sphinx of Egypt. Now we all know Cleo and a Caesar were dating for a while before Marc Antony, and it is historic fact that Rome loved to travel conquering the world as it roamed.

***Morning Moon***

I saw the moon this morning, full and bold
A golden hue it threw off as
Clouds drifted by
Was that a face, are you watching?
The man in the moon not a children's tale
As he turned his head, looked around at me, really
Perception of the early hours, how interesting, free

A straggler car, no traffic yet
Snow dots here and there, soon gone
But by our favorite witch-dramas we've seen
Orangey-autumn sky, lending a film of gold
Has significance to those who can read it
I can't recall, was it an omen, trouble coming?
But it wasn't blood viscously
I'll not worry at all, what or why.

I looked back at you as I walked on by
I thought "hello moon", then "morning moon, but for you
That's right; for me I've just risen, so I should say good night"
But the moon doesn't sleep; it doesn't care
What's going on down here or anywhere
It'll orbit until later, always the same face
Never showing me his dark side, keeping a glow
As phases begin, now waning in space

# AN ELEVATOR IN ISTANBUL

I LIVED IN ISTANBUL FOR ALMOST TWO YEARS AS A TEACHER OF ENGLISH AS A FOREIGN LANGUAGE – WHAT FOLLOWS ARE NOTES FROM A JOURNAL I KEPT DURING MY TIME THERE

***First Impressions / Year One:***

I'm told Istanbul is a Third World country. OK, it's a Third World and everyone's on a cell phone. What kind of third world is that? And, this one here has his polo hoodie up mimicking his MTV idols. When did we cross into first world? Maybe, just maybe it's Cool World; the starring actress didn't have the chest breadth for the role she played but this place certainly does.

International TV stations here can be fun with the stations being plentiful and in a variety of languages. So far, I've seen the "Return of the King" and "Spiderman" in German; although, it didn't hold the same momentum for me when Peter Parker was atop a building trying to get his spider web to shoot. His comments just didn't hold the same humorous effect, or should I say a different kind of humorous effect.

I've seen varieties of movies dubbed in Turkish but lips don't seem to follow the script. "Armageddon" was classic tamam, tamam.

When the Turkish team scores a goal horns blare in the streets. If they win a game shots are fired in the air and I'm talking from real guns that so many seem to have in their possession. It's best to stay in and watch from home.

It's cloudy a lot here but today; nonetheless, the sun is trying to shine through: silly sun or always faithful? I'm glad something is until we cause it to explode. Can we cause it to go dim? No, I'm going with always faithful or trust the way it is.

My first experience of one of "those" cabdrivers happened. We had been warned at a teacher's meeting about an abduction trend among certain cab drivers. A couple of the teachers had been robbed and left. I got lucky with this one.

I used my usual survival Turkish directions and interjections but he insisted on talking to me in a snarly kind of way. He suddenly turned onto a ramp, darted on the highway, off the highway, in and around the side streets, overshooting my destination making the trip 8 ytl instead of the usual 3. I was watching where he was going very closely which seemed to cause him concerned surprise. He didn't want me to get out of the cab as he went to talk to a friend of his (another cabbie) after he finally stopped on the street all cabs congregate and leave from. He wanted me to pay him 20 ytl, the change from which I'd never have known again; although, it could have been interesting to witness his miracle of ytl at 8:20 odds. I called my son while he was out of the cab then got out myself and handed him the cell. I watched closely as he spoke with my son, I wasn't about to take my eyes off my cell. He handed the phone back to me. We drove to the nearby mall, I got out and my son came out and paid him the 8 lira. He tried to say I wasn't sure where I wanted to go. Liar! I don't know what my son said to him but it was inspirational to say the least.

If I never meet another cabbie like him again it won't hurt my feelings at all.

*At The Language Academy Ranch*:

It's interesting being judged by students who don't speak the language I'm teaching, and who wouldn't know whether or not I'm a good teacher who's fluent in my language or not, if their lives depended on it. Many times their epiphanies of learning were simply answers copied from the answer key and when that answer is no longer in reach there is withdrawal with big smiles and "I don't understand". How can that be when you just said you did?

Students in general, but especially beginners, should not be given answer keys; it's just bad business. This school uses the availability of answer keys with the text as a marketing ploy. That's a wrong approach. It makes being stuck in the back with a double-edge sword as encouragement to walk the plank preferable. Pick a killer whale with its mouth already open.

*A universal aside*: Toilet paper as tissue, the wrong end but suit yourself. There's always tissue as toilet paper but in that case you're doing your backside a favor or is it considered prestigious because the tissues cost more?

*A Relaxing Cup Of Joe*:

It just doesn't feel right. There's music on the balcony at Starbucks but the traffic is so loud I can't hear. At least they are consistent with their coffee, something that Dunkin' Donuts fails at here. I've never tasted anything so bad.

*Sublime Though*t: Existentialist and mystical fast food lunches leave one as empty as the places of origin. It's right to dump on the bad and jeans aren't too tight but I'd rather live than contemplate what is existence.

The sun almost shone bright today. It did happen.

*Observations and Tastes:* Olive oil is good, chocolate – eh, dried fruits and nuts abundant. Hamburgers are lamb Joe's (as opposed to sloppy) and lamb's throats are slit in the streets in celebration of the slaughter; the streets can be rather messy. Cheeses are the bomb; what a wondrous variety. Yogurt is outstanding. My son has friends in Italy who ask him to bring them yogurt when he comes to visit and Italy is the place to go for great food.

*The Police Here Carry Automatic Weaponry:* I am not particularly inspired by the police station. It went very smoothly with someone who speaks Turkish.

*As I Venture Out On My Own:* A ride on the Bosphorus and did I almost get picked up? It's hard to tell in Turkish. He asked if I was Italian, I think, or was it Anatolian, Cappadocian, that's the other place. He said, "English, no Turkish" when he saw my book and I said "yeah, Italian-American". I don't speak Italian. He wanted to go to the shady part of the boat but I was there for the sun. Then he made sign language for 'give me your phone number". I said, "What for? You can't speak English." I'd rather get a tan if I can.

The guy at Starbucks who wants to practice his English wanted to take me to the Islands on a tour so he could talk. "Can I have your phone number?" Well, no actually and after he brought me my white chocolate mocha latte. Now I'll probably never get good service. Meanwhile: the crew back at Starbucks in Bakırköy were stumped when I asked them to ice my macchiato. I deprived them of talking about me in front of me in a foreign language I didn't speak yet by walking away in a samba after telling them to forget it. Now whom is he going to roll his eyes about? I sure don't know.

*Afterthought*: Did the young guy want to stab me and take my wallet on the shady side of the boat, which takes away from cool shade and throws a diabolical light on it? Now I have to wonder: Do they ask for your phone number when they want to stab you in Turkey?

Someone spoke English to me tonight. Nice neighbors.

Grandma as the con in her pretty purple print dress, I just don't need that many tissues, but when I see her I'll buy them. She's one of the people that lends that special character to the town.

*A Mayor's Wife Who Sends A Car:* My private S. takes her test so I'll write I guess. It's not the same as Starbucks but those guys aggravated me anyway. I'll get back there sooner or later. I wonder if should check schedules to avoid people of course. I want to meet up with you – not. S. does so well with understanding innuendo lately although she can't get it out of her mouth sometimes. We'll keep working on that.

*Practicing English:* My beginner class decided to take me out to dinner. We went to this place by the shore and I was impressed by how noisy it was. They weren't the least bit disturbed by it, in fact to them, it was as if there weren't noise at all. I got a phone call and had difficulty hearing my son who wanted to ensure I was ok. The PKK, an in-house terrorist group, had blown up a few shops in the square near to where he lives, and he was concerned the students had taken me to one of the local restaurants. I assured him we were a safe distance away. The next day I took a walk through the square. The PKK wanted to make a statement only so there wasn't as much damage as could have been, but there was just enough.

*Don't Mention It:* My roommate who deserves no mention has stooped to new lows. Peeping through bedroom keyholes wasn't enough, now it's the bathroom and wiping his backside with the toilet brush. All I can come up with is what a tool (a word that wasn't popular then when I was writing this but it is now). Major L for LOSER, give me an L, give me an O, give me an SER – what's that spell? Believe it or not, the name of someone that contains only 3 letters. (And as I sit here reading this over remembering that guy, I can't remember his name, which stood for something beautiful like sea or dolphin, but he wasn't.)

After reflecting, thinking, and giving up, his name came to me as I was waking from sleep this morning, Ido, which in Istanbul is the name of the sea bus company that uses the image of a dolphin as its logo: Istanbul Deniz Otobüsleri.

I feel happy today, an epiphany, breakthrough, coming together or am I dying of a rare fatal disease? Some days nothing's good enough. Anyway, my student will have a good holiday because he scored high and the others will do well. I can feel it.

*Stay tuned if you care to. I'm just getting started.*

*Here's an addendu*m: In a word, Rakı (spelled with the "funny" i, the one that's not dotted, so it has an "ih" sound.)

Rakı is a traditional liquor, similar to Ouzo or Sambuca, that can be drunk two ways: one straight up of course and the other diluted with water. When water is added it turns the liquid a cloudy white and is referred to as "bulls milk". I tried it both ways and prefer it straight. The one quality, I noticed, about Rakı that stands out is similar to how alcohols relax the body, this one dulls the mind. I've described it to my students as 'it makes you stupid'. (I'd never drink Rakı on a school night, let me tell you.) They've laughed out loud at that knowing too well its effects. I also have a cool person, unusual woman reputation because I drink it straight, (I think the water spoils the taste) which makes me... I don't know... like I'm tough because I can handle it. Really, I'm just trying to blend and pay my respects to the culture.

One evening a bunch of us were out, or it was the night I turned everyone on to an international food fest at the house (see what I mean) and the Rakı was flowing. I didn't have to teach the next day - good thing - anyway, I tried to put a wash on and couldn't get the machine to start. I checked the outlet, reset the dials, made sure the door was shut and was completely baffled. I ran across the street to the school (convenient right) and grabbed the guy in the office for assistance. He looked at the machine, reached out, pushed the machine door, it clicked closed and the wash cycle started. We looked at each other and I said, "no more Rakı". He thought that was the greatest; needless to say everyone knew about it and my cool reputation got even cooler, but I might find another way to blend and stay alert.

### *Getting To Know You Continues On*

*1 July 2006*

I jumped a train! Son of a B----, which is what I said when I couldn't pull the door open and wasn't up to riding on the outside until the first stop. It was at Eminönü's train station.

I never considered the strength it took to open the door against its will (or anything else a stuntman does for that matter). The young boys who do this regularly pull the doors open as if it's effortless and many times they ride holding on from the outside. (Here's where I should let you know these trains are leftover reprobates from WWll; it's like riding in hollowed out tin cans, rickety and rattling, that make these stunts possible at all. There are posters around depicting new, luxury trains that'll be there... someday.)

I had made it back to the station just at the last minute and the train began to pull out. I thought, "I'm not missing this one" and turned to find an opened door but first I ran to a car in an attempt to pull doors open. No way were they budging. That was a revelation in itself. I looked back and saw doors that had stayed open so I slowed my running, let the car catch up to me and jumped in slamming back into the poor soul who was standing against the back of the car near the door. Although I'd grabbed the rail along the back of the last seat to swing in and perfect my landing, I 'boofed' into him anyway, which is exactly what he said as I knocked some wind out of him. Point of physics: although I stopped moving the train didn't, it brought me right up to par. I looked back at him, as I got my feet under me and began walking to a seat, with the biggest smile on my face. It was exhilarating and turned my legs to jelly at the same time. When I sat down, I doubled over laughing to myself but I was filled with such glee, when I picked my head up and looked around, the few men in the car were all smirking too, especially the one I'd made contact with. I doubled over again laughing to myself. "I did it!"

It was awesome although I'll never do it again! I enjoyed the lesson in physics. Reflecting more soberly, I believe I'd never make it as a stunt man, but I can't say it wouldn't be a fascinating job.

I saw a Jaguar creeping bumper-to-bumper down the street seeming out of place in desolation. (This is not a particularly ritzy part of town. A car like that definitely draws attention to itself. I succumbed with the other street-side gapers.) Some do-gooders have suggested I should get a boyfriend while I'm here. I wonder if there's a shop at the mall. I'd browse but that's about it. Right now, at this stage, that would be like having a ball and chain around my neck to keep me perpetually drowning. My imagination isn't good enough to know how I'd manage that. In a spirit of positivity, I'll put on my to do list to rethink my thinking. I'm being fair and that could take a considerable amount of time. I like that. Go team me.

It's the 3rd not the 4th but my independence was a couple of days ago. Cool, windy and gray, a beautiful day.

*7 July*

Fleeting and I can't remember what I wanted to write, but I did find out it's not that I'm American; it's Turkish people, something told to me by a Turkish person. (My son has good Turkish friends who proudly tell me anything I need to know about their culture.) So, when the man knocked me off the sidewalk and I landed on my backside, and no one was interested in helping me up; although a couple of people looked back as I looked up and called. "thank-you" after the man and smiled, it had nothing to do with nationality. They do it to each other. I blend.

*An aside – way-deep thought*: The US trains the best terrorists and then it's a bear to find them because we taught them that too.

*Deeper yet*: Was uncivilized what I was going to write? Has that been the word I couldn't think of, the thing I couldn't put my finger on? But, that is rightly so. My son's friend defined it. I cannot describe what's wrong and in this day and age, in this century, I never would have considered not civilized. Aren't we all by now? So, is Third World uncivilized with so many reserved, genteel people? There are many crowded into the space that is Istanbul lending a much better chance for all kinds. Even when I thought, "it's like the wild west with technology and cars", uncivilized never crossed my mind.

List things to do to keep busy. You are alive; besides, there's kontors and simits.

Things unspoken I wanted to say emerged from where they lie today. Best left that way. Find peace as ashes fly.

Cappuccino is tea here and it's amazing how many people are in line for Pirates. They run in knocking each other over similar to 'like they drive and have accidents'. A man tried to knock me out of the way to get in with his two small children. Please, after you and ouch. A lot of young people are out. The brown sugar cubes are in strange shapes. Tea is the national beverage served in small glasses so you could burn your fingers if not for the saucer, but I really didn't want tea. Nescafé is king of coffees. At a café, seeing I was the only one there, the barista thought Nescafé and froth could be passed off as a Cappuccino so the espresso machine wouldn't have to be used and then cleaned – it's more practical to wait until there's a crowd so use is more economical. Besides, as an outsider I wouldn't know that difference – not.

*As July marches on:*

I came close to getting run over and I wasn't taking a chance. There were no cars but a bus was about to turn the corner, so, of course I ran. A truck came from the opposite direction flying with no intention to slow and I was almost completely across the street. I jumped out of its way and onto the curb.

But I already knew it doesn't matter where you walk. Compact cars and motorcycles have pulled up behind me on the sidewalk to get around traffic and to park. It's a very different sensation, let's say it's an eerie feeling, when you realize there's a car behind you and not on the road. No place is safe.

Learn English but damn the culture. Can you have what's best without taking the culture to heart? That's part of the problem or is the problem. Take the language without what makes the language. It's not a democracy. Note to self: I'm going to have to work on not falling in love with my classes.

What good are dictionaries? For "take away" it's çalmak but that meant nothing to the waiter. But, from “take” the waiter told me “paket”. Now, that makes sense to my canted English brain as “pack-it”. And that makes sense.

*August now:*

A week ago I was crop-dusted. That’s the best way to describe it as I was sitting at a furniture store/café and a truck drove by with what looked like a great deal of smoke from it’s exhaust. Way too much smoke, in fact. My student laughed and said it was for snakes and gestured to the air. I realized it was for insects. How unhealthy is this?

Ok, what a great day! I had an actual half-hour by the shore with a minor intrusion by a sketchy man who wanted sex, how sadly 60s. A hopeless romantic sleaze, damn the language barrier, let’s just do it! A future linguist himself who understood, beyond doubt by the colorful language I used in response, that I’d rather not take him up on his offer. Expletives are universal.

Movie, dinner, and a blessed shower after a great walk and another sleaze driving a car, trying to follow me from the grocery store. The glare works as he slithered, car and all, around the corner and I hid away.

Too good lookin’ at 51 or are these poor fellows that hard up. How did that go, “demented and sad, but social”? Plus, pathetic and animal making uncivilized ring true.

It’s not the 60s. There was a passion and drugged love about it. This is bland and emotionless, no flavor, no salt, no sweetness, no, empty and missing, not exciting, not even desperate. Any of those would be substance, but this is sex without feeling. How do you manage that? Don’t answer.

The man at the shore was indignant. He grumbled back wanting me to know I had a problem with me for not complying, trying to get and keep my attention as he walked away. Should I be scared? I must separate from it. I hear there are many lewd men around but anyone who has power or thinks they have power over another exercises it. The kindest, gentlest people lose it in these circumstances. Who knows who’s telling the truth.

My son read me the riot act on this one. I will only return to that place during peak hours. Worse could have befallen. He's lived here longer; he would know.

### ***As Darkness Begins To Fall On Istanbul And Me***

*Still the 12th of August*

Capitalism in Turkey doesn't exist, but some say to steal, lie and cheat is the same as in the U.S. They've got a hell of an impression. Even the most learned can be non-fluent and miss what's going on.

The lawlessness here is the same as how the law is carried out in New York; a car that is stolen is not as important as a murder. For the sake of the car it is better to let your insurance take care of it – you'll get a new car back faster than it would take the law to catch the thief (thieves) who are running their own business and who can prime a car just as fast or faster than any pit crew. The law is working on this; however, they don't want their cars stolen either. Darn those murders, kidnappings, beatings (those who commit assault), hold-ups (ha – robbers), and even drugged-drunk driving drivers who get in the way. Then there's prostitutes, pimps, dealers, molesters… oops, almost forgot rapists. My apologies to those criminals I left out.

We care enough that it almost kills us; here they kill each other because no one cares if they do. Opposites attract?

Sure that's the same. How could I have missed it?

*A Lesson in Contractioning:*

If I have 80 hours per 4 weeks, that's 20 hours per week. I must be available for up to 40 hours per week and can work 50 + hours per week but that's overtime unless after a 60 hour work week your hours are cut back and given to people who get paid less, then it becomes per month and overtime is anything over 80 hours for the month, so, the overtime you worked is lost and not secure. Money and expertise have fraudulently been made use of and stolen. That is aligned with good American business, but companies in the U.S. like that find themselves investigated and out of business.

If we could have a little of the U.S. here, that wouldn't be that bad.

Five o'clock call to prayer and I think of Ethel Merman (not mermaid), anyway – I used to like the Liturgy of the Hours, but I thought Vespers was a little later, maybe not. These were the shorter prayers – the long ones in the morning and evening. How special to read the priests' prayer book, I thought. How many excommunicated me for being unholy because I'd been divorced and bounced me between old and new testament to support their judgement. (There were one or two who forgave me.)

Not so special then.

Only man would think of a throwing bull chips contest. Bulls wouldn't touch the stuff.

Bulls can hold a throwing stools contest, those round disks with four legs and dowels they can catch up in their horns and give a whirl.

*13th Aug*

Things to do to stay positive: one: turn off brain… sometimes I think that's happened.

Get up and stretch, welcome the sun (that's how it'll be encouraged to shine), organize things, go for a power walk, read a book you enjoy and take notes, erase anyone else's empty assumptions written in the margins, ignore what is read into the simple beauty of a direct statement.

(If Freud had something to do with it he would've mentioned Freud's name.)

My flat mate as I stand corrected because roommate carries connotations in Great Britain (says who), who deserves no mention topped the charts for inane statements with his brother, the visitor who will never leave, giving him a close second. Only a rocket scientist could have possibly known that an oversized bottle of soda would not allow the fridge door to shut properly. When I thanked him in a hostile tone because my food had gone bad in the warmed icebox, he replied, "It's the school's fault". "The school's fault?" "You know this fridge since May. It works the same way." "That's right, see"… at which point I asked him to go back to his room or wear the spoiled food.

During a time of emergency, when the power went out, again, and I noticed his brother on the phone, I walked toward him and asked, "Are you calling someone to help? I have a number of a guy who will come and check things out…" "No this phone is on credit and it's out of credit."

Later on he ranted, "I helped you! You… you wanted to use my phone!"
I guess so.

Something positive at any rate:
Keep going and teach. Enjoy this wonderful student, a good eye for comparison and detail – a good accountant.

Look forward to enjoying the peacefulness of the night.

Getting bird poop on you as one or more fly overhead is supposed to be good luck. I don't know, we'll have to see. You can't say the sun doesn't shine here.

I'm tired enough I guess. I flattened the end of my pen for the sake of the CD, now maybe some peaceful sleep. It could happen.

*22nd Aug - Early*

I wonder if the way I think is to do with menopause. I can't say I'm irrational because it's the way I think when I think (deem) something as important.

I wanted my daughter here; I wanted us together and now to work out the rest:

So, 1 – call L
2 – call Ist – G
3 – contact Nur.
4 - contact W
5 - contact N
6 – contact P in

… And write this all on a separate sheet to take with – now go to sleep and stop freaking. You are in a beautiful place; make the best of what's there.

7 – search local schools and make it positive.

*21 September*

I slept through the call to prayer – thank God.
It stopped raining long enough so I could get somewhere bone dry.
Thanks again.

It's not easy sleeping through a call to prayer if you're not used to hearing them, but what's worse is trying to sleep through the call to rise before sunup during the special month of fasting when all must eat and then cannot break the fast before sunset. When the time comes to break the fast there is a countdown on TV like the ball being dropped New Year's Eve in Times Square. To rise, in a particular town I was residing temporarily, people marched through he streets banging on or banging together pots and pans. I remember dreaming about drumming and slowly becoming conscious realizing what was taking place. First thought of the day, "you're kidding me…" I did find out this isn't done everywhere. Thank God for that.

***Behind The Scenes Of "As Darkness Begins To Fall…"***

In case there were any raised eyebrows about what school or who is this flatmate deserving no mention: you've probably picked up on the fact I don't as a rule name names specifically and I change names to protect the guilty or just because. (I think there are clues enough that you might be able to put 2 and 2 together, possibly coming up with 5.) Anyway, darkness falling isn't negative but change as in Autumn from Summer or the day becoming night, night becoming day. My time was wrapping up in Istanbul for now (or then). I did go back, if you've read "An Apartment In Madrid" you'd know when, which I will title as 'Take 2' when the time comes around to post. For right now here's some notes, more accurately two emails, from a communication between me and other teachers, administrators, et. al. who hosted a website about problematic places to avoid teaching and working if you're from out of town. Of course, you never find out about these things when you're looking. It's related for the most part to "As Darkness Begins to Fall On Istanbul And Me", and as it turned out, this school in particular was notoriously known:

*The First Communication:*

"Here's the skinny on “The School”: it is simply another company (owned by Ayko - a construction company if I have that straight) that is using a company with a name known for quality, to make a buck or many YTL in this case. Management is awful, “The Director” has outright insulted the US and New York, my place of birth at the teacher meetings, I have experienced him violently scream during a meeting like he's always wanted to be the best Stasi, which is why he went to the US for his education to begin with, and many of the teachers have difficulty getting their pay, and, as the students say, 'for example':

One evening the pay was late, “The Director” was the messenger boy and he was so busy prior that he couldn't take the time to check the envelope to verify all the pay was there. I had hurried from where I was to the office for the sake of my manager, who had called me, and thought she would get to go home after she paid the teachers. When I arrived I was told by “Him” 'oh well, so the pay's not here... I sent so-and-so back to Taksim to get it and you'll be paid in a couple of hours or you can get it tomorrow.' This meant the manager had to stay and the teachers had to stay past when the classes ended to wait to get their pay that was already two days late because payday fell on a Saturday.

There are other things that have happened to do with pay, like “The School” refusing to acknowledge the change on the YTL exchange rate, which was noted to me in order to get me to sign the contract that it would be taken care of, I had nothing to concern about. What is interesting is that in the contract, although it can not be written out in a euro or us dollar and YTL format, it is stated in English and Turkish if you do not give 30 days notice prior to quitting, they will take 500 US dollars (in my case being from the US) as a penalty. That takes care of the exchange rate from their angle and is a lot of YTL. Ayko otherwise will not sign a contract with a teacher.

I had to wait months for a flat that I was supposed to get in less than two weeks after I had signed the contract, and I wound up with a real low-life flat mate on top of it. “The School” has no interest in doing anything about it."

*The Second:*

"Here's the final chapter of "The School" and me. I had given notice and was winding up my time with a wonderful private student who just wanted to learn English. She studied, utilized her lessons and made it evident that she could use what was learned from her previous level. Everything was good.

Came the time to fill out my time sheet with lessons taught, oral tests given and this time I lost hours for about a two week period because of student vacations and so on. (I am full time so I am guaranteed hours, I was told 20 hours a week but I was to make myself available for up to 40 hours a week and, my first pay and subsequent pays were always based on what I did weekly.) I reminded "The School" like I was supposed to that I was falling under 20 hours per week and my office manager smiled at me and said, "so, you are full time so you get paid". The first part of the month I was still working a lot of overtime. I was at 50 hours a week. I listed the hours owed on a separate line like I did when I had to list travel time and such. I got the time card in early in case there were questions or problems.

A few days from payday the HR manager, a professional liar by trade, called and asked me what the hours under 'The School contract' were all about. After I responded he said that I wasn't guaranteed 20 hours a week but 80 hours a month. My pay had never been calculated this way up to that point. I said "what are you saying" and he side stepped around the conversation to it wasn't necessary for me to list my hours because they would take care of it. I calculated my pay each month, I always knew what I got and I said, "as long as it comes out the same". It didn't and I was shorted a mite over 300 YTL.

What this means is they are a lawless organization that changes the rules that don't really exist when they choose it be that way, without concern for consequence. The overtime that is worked is not secure. A teacher's list of duties is broken down by week. When it comes to pay, "The Director" does what he wants. If he were simply a control freak, "The School" would be a nice place to work. They 100 percent fraudulently represented themselves which is what they do to everyone as I found out from another teacher just coming on board. I gave her the skinny on them and wished her luck. Another friend who is starting his own business, an internet language / translation organization, and who will be leaving them soon himself, was promised a full time contract if he quit his part time position and just worked for "The School". He said ok and they didn't give him a contract.

They owe me over 1000 YTL from the exchange that hasn't yet been and won't ever be acknowledged. If you choose to work for "The School" I'd keep in close contact with your Embassy."

***Here's One Of Those Clues I'd Mentioned:***
*Addendum: Everybody Loves Idioms:*

*(Abducted from 'Where Do You Think You Get It From' - "Be Resilient, Try Things, Check The World Out)*

One of my students had asked me, "How can that be, people in New York are awake 24-hours a day with no rest? If the city never sleeps then no one sleeps. People have to sleep." She said it almost angrily as if that's a desired trait and why can't she do it! No one else in the class had any ideas on it (according to Berlitz they were second level - beginners first class); a lesson in defining "what's a shift"and idiomatic expression, "the city never sleeps" was due and happened next. I assured her and the rest of the class people sleep the same as they do; like a hospital, if an establishment stays open all night, different people work there different times of the day to keep it open, so in a nutshell, (oops, there's another idiom) a city, any city that boasts it's a city that "never sleeps" means if you can't sleep there's always something to do to pass the time; many places stay open 24/7, 24 hours a day for 7 days a week. (We didn't get into cab availability or bus and subway schedules, nor into the fact that if you are there between 4 and 6 A.M., most likely there'll be maintenance going on. After all, the place needs to be cleaned and kept up.) I realized New York City has quite a reputation! It's a supernatural place of wonderment.

***No Elevator Yet: Take 2***

*July of a New Year*

After 3 showers there was still hot water to spare; my son lives in a good spot. This lends hope to elevators; they'll be building them soon – I can feel it. Then again, you can't argue with good cardio.

*Sublime Reflection After Living In 3 Other Countries And Braving All the Airports Intertwined:*

We have to make things tough because of terrorists and their terrorism. I'm a foreigner – Italian, Swiss, British, and Native American – who is for the most part European. My Italian Grandfather who moved to the United States about 100 years ago makes me no less Italian, but depending on the circumstances and when he became a U.S. citizen, I may or may not be granted an E.U. passport. A terrorist with an EU passport has no problems.

No country can seem to get a handle on security.

*Extended Sublime Reflection*

Lurches: A gaggle of tall butlers.

*Continuing into August*

A muse over coffee at Starbucks: Iron and Coffee or Breakfast at Tiffany's? Think about it. Why did I? Don't know, it just came to me...

Gloria Jean's gives good coffee too.

*It Could Be Funny, Sad and Terrifying (there's that word again):*

The drawback of dictators no matter how good their intentions: "Let ***Me*** tell *You* what we're gonna do…"

*As the Muse Continues*

How interesting to be back and how much like home it is. Istanbul, now my old friend; there are no surprises but only the things that I knew and I know my way around appreciating the new developments. There's the bread guy to see again and the cheese shop down the street my son goes to. The fish guy is down a block, around the corner – I remember he wanted me to work with him so he could teach me Turkish and I could teach him English - all so friendly and familiar, and Migros, super MMM Migros will be wonderful to shop at again. The square has its simit vendors and the teacher store down at the end on the left, Beyaz Adam Kitabevi, before you cross the street to the mall is the best place for absolutely all needs. The school I'll be teaching at, temporarily at least, is right across the way from it; we see people going in and out and performing death defying acts to get across the street through the traffic. How my perspective has changed now that there's no fear but a welcome familiarity. It hasn't gotten less crowded; that's how it goes. After all this it'll be interesting to see how New York City comes across; will I find it too crowded anymore?

*Muezzins and...*

Call to prayer or churches having conversations with bells; contrasting Italy and Istanbul. While I walked, I'd heard roosters crow around mid-day boasting about the night's escapades and conquests, something I never heard in Istanbul, but there were cats and the town dogs working together keeping the rat population down. That is teamwork! Walking along the shore I'd sometimes see kittens, who'd spied well-rounded pigeons, crouched to pounce, the bird so much larger and I'd wonder, "Can you swim?" It made for an interesting vision.

*September - Not easy but not impossible*

How to learn Turkish from daily-living communication and visualizing what's being said - the following, from doodling one fateful day, turned out to be an advanced Turkish lesson according to me. And the doodle goes on as you can see. I'd recommend trying this at home. In it's title is the first letter of the town I lived at the time:

***Gardening in B-Town***

"Bahçesi is garden of
Good vegetables for you
Bahçe is too, flower garden in bloom
Parchesi is thirsty or
Parçesi in Turkish (only a Turk would know)
Parcheesie a game
How do you spell parcheesey,

Parçeezi, par-cheesey
Not at all chessey
Good griefi, not griefee
Nor griefy no, maybe
Oil on pizza pie to go

Pizzahçesi, pizza garden
Pizzahçesi, will it possibly sell
Pizza Bahçe, Pizzabahçe
The best marketing I'll insist
Or maybe Pizzabahcé with a French twist
Kahvebahçesi a coffee garden
Never heard of one of those
Subahçesi water garden or
Beach by Black Sea, by Marmara
The Bosphorus, a place of water falls
Currents collide, dolphins chatter with glee

Ekmekçesi, Ekbahçesimek
A bread garden of rolls
Ekmekbahçe
Kaiser, sub-sandwich
Lavaş or Pida
Lamacunbahçesi or
A garden of lamacun
Traditional baking you'll have to come try
The pizza of Turkey
Istanbulian cuisine
Istanbulbahçesi
A garden of people make a rolling
Sea wave of heads walking
In the square ahead of me
The road I can't now see
How is it we all fit?
Just how can it be?

Bar Bahçesi or Barçesi
Could we use a drink now?
Paşabahçe is glassware

Ç – ch, ş – sh, ţ – th
Doesn't exist
Beţany, baţ, birţ, worţ
Nah, not used to this, but fun if it did
Merhababahçesi, too many syllables
Merhababa and her thieves
Make it his responsibility
That sounds good to me
Merhabahçesi, a garden of hellos
Or a very big welcome
From mymerhaba.com a
Good site to go

Goodbyebahçesi, not the yellow brick road
No gardens there that I know
Hoşça Kal Bahçesi, stay pleasantly garden
Or Garden of Eden
Utopia of sin when
Slithery and slimy neighbors move in
Utopiabahçe
Well, there went the hoodbahçesi, it's no more
Or the neighborhood garden, barriobahçesi
Does that invasion exist?
Did those two worlds collide?

But what I was thinking in Goodbye Bahçesi
A Bed and Breakfast as I'm just passing through
Hoşça Kal Bahçesi or Hoşça Kal Bahçe
That the sun always shine on you"

(I could write greeting cards)

Nobody*'s perfect to say the least; one of those encounters that no one ever heard of happening:*

I went walking one day as I do and was followed by a funny little man. What he thought I was or who I was I can't say but he came up behind me and was either trying to hold my hand or steal my bracelet. Not making use of the pocket Turkish dictionary I usually carry around, I let him have it verbally in plain English that I didn't appreciate what had just happened. He stood quietly, looked at me and as I turned to walk away slapped me – what we'd call "upside the head" – which really made me mad. I glared at him and said, "YOU HIT ME…" then proceeded with more verbiage. I wanted to swing back but the thought that he might be carrying a weapon came to mind. My son had told me about someone who tried to talk a man out of abusing his girlfriend in public and was stabbed by the abusing boyfriend who'd concealed a knife. I kept my space, snapped open my cell, which he tried to knock out of my hand but I was so focused on him I saw it coming, kept dialing and swung my hand back, as if the move was choreographed, so he couldn't reach it. At that point he turned and walked away. I was trembling but followed him and as I lucked out, my son answered and kept talking to me until I calmed down. The funny little man kept looking back, then disappeared into the crowd.

Speaking to my son caused a ripple effect: his wife, her family, friends, no one understood why such a thing would happen. I was assured that type of thing is unusual, lucky me. The most fun part of the whole thing was when I shared my experience with a fellow teacher I lived with. She's a tiny woman with a fiery temper and was ready to go back out so we could find the guy and let him have it. I tried to wrap my head around the thought and was overcome with the helpless reality that as crowded as Istanbul is, and of course the area I lived, it would genuinely be easier to find a needle in a haystack. Without actually knowing who he was, there'd be no way we'd find him, but we could have made it a night of pub hopping had we gone out.

It didn't discourage me at any rate. I'd lived here a year previously and, true, this type of thing doesn't usually happen. Either way, we're good.

As Ap*ril Approached:*

*Cheers To Flatmates!*

Don't be helpful I think, but I thought too late as I gathered up the pile of lesson plans and homework into a bag and look down on a few pages stuck together with second-hand prophylactics. Well, I'm not touching those as I lifted from the edge and a spent contraception packet slips from between, "all of you into the bag" with the last of the homework, ungraded.

The floor is clean as I muse, “I guess she doesn’t want children”, although, I didn’t find any insect repellent and fly swatters. “Back! Back away, you may not enter the gate!” The job is done and soon it’ll be my turn to organize and pack, only I won’t leave my room this way.

I have to say I’ll miss my bidets although I prefer the Europeanism of temperature control. At least they have them in Turkey, but I guess cold water only is punishment for being human. Or, is it humane?

*I'm off to become a grandma! I'll be back again someday. Maybe there'll be more elevators. I can feel it, there will be. Fear not cardio, we’ll work it out. Here’s something I’ll miss either way:*

***A Ferry Heading To Beşiktaş***

Seagulls argue over simits
Boof into each other as they glide
Reaching for the same piece
CAW – UFF
Beg your pardon
Cawf-it-awf, pick up speed, fly

White-faced ducks bob and watch
Catching what drops in the sea
Seeming unmoved
Tilt up on their heads
Staying under much longer than me

The birds are reason just enough
To buy crusted, gold-rounded breads
Half the fun is to share
Ask any child who is there
Gulls keep to ship’s side and aft for the ride
With what is tossed in the air

# Afterword: Notes From Madrid - Behind The Scenes At The Academy

This will be of particular interest, like clues to a puzzle, if you've read or are reading "An Apartment In Madrid." Of course, names have been changed to protect the guilty or are we all innocent in our own way:

## ***Skeletons In The Closet Of The Apartment In Madrid***

*Lederhosen and Mr. Belushi*

The petty cash was in Mr. Belushi's charge and he was broke. "Oh well", he yawned, "I'm broke." The next day it was rumored someone had lifted the petty cash, probably some broke student. Get Lederhosen and Mr. Belushi on the case!

Mr. Belushi was 1&1/2 hours late for his language class. "Well, I was hungry", he yawned, "and you know how the metro is."

*Mr. Belushi In the Land Of The Free*

One evening when Lederhosen and Mr. Belushi were still in the land of the free, Lederhosen had been asleep when he was awakened by a dragging and thump sound around 3A.M. He grabbed a flail from his collection of medieval weapons in a chest at the foot of his bed. As he approached the bathroom cautiously, he spied Mr. Belushi leaning toward the medicine cabinet mirror with his tongue hanging out. Lederhosen dropped the flail and leaned on the doorway molding. Not looking away from the mirror Mr. Belushi asked, "Is my tongue cracked?" "No", Lederhosen replied, "It's just wide".

*Fly Me To the Land Of Franco*

Mr. Belushi was groggy as usual and spilled his water on another passenger's seat on the plane. "Oops", he said when she returned from the toilet. "I put a blanket over it." The plane was filled to capacity so she couldn't change her seat. Although she changed blankets periodically, she had a chilly backside for most of the 8-hour flight.

*4 Months Later*

Mr. Belushi stepped out on his own with Mr. Tall and some other guy. They were drinking, carrying on, being loud about the fact they were teachers, but they forgot to get their passports renewed and didn't have paperwork anyway.

"Dear Mom", Mr. Belushi wrote, "I'll be home again soon. I was thrown out of the country for being rowdy. Thank goodness they didn't find out I was selling pot to some of my other friends. Can I have my old room back? - B"

Lederhosen was at Oktoberfest dancing with the dirndl.

*Mr. Belushi Over There*

She, one of the partners, went to the states to see Mr. Belushi because he got thrown out of the country she was trying to exploit with the other two owners of the academy. They were so in love she knew Mr. Belushi would marry her. She returned to her old job a month later. Being in the land of the free Mr. Belushi had no more problems; his future wife wasn't anywhere nearby.

*Mr. Belushi Starts Thinking*

One day, Mr. Belushi decided to come back to Madrid for a visit. His future wife wanted to see him too, tragic, tragic. Mr. Belushi thought he might fly to the country next door and saunter over the border, besides, they make good port wine there. "What if I was just out for a walk and I crossed over the border", Mr. Belushi mused. "Would anyone really notice?"

*The Rental Agent*

Lederhosen and Mr. Belushi had a friend who was a rental agent. She was a very pretty South-American living in Madrid with long legs, so they didn't worry about her political beliefs, whether she realized them or not.

She always robbed from everybody to give to herself. This time she was stealing from another friend of Lederhosen and Mr. Belushi who didn't have legs as long and was a little older, but she was sort-of-sexy.

The rental agent thought she was clever by writing about what she was doing in Spanish to the older friend of Lederhosen and Mr. Belushi who was sort-of-sexy, because she couldn't speak Spanish that well, but what she didn't think about was that the sort-of-sexy friend of Lederhosen and Mr. Belushi could read. "Thanks for the confession", the sort-of-sexy friend replied to the email. "Muy bien and mucho gracias."

*Inside The Academy*

The academy that Lederhosen and Mr. Belushi used to attend was a business associate of the agent with long legs. The older friend who was sort-of-sexy told the academy that the rental agent was stealing from her. "Emmm – errr" was all they would say. "We can't make her pay you. We just let her do business with us. We don't make any money, she does."

"Hmmmm" thought the sort-of-sexy friend of Lederhosen and Mr. Belushi. "The rental agent said she has to work for them and doesn't make any money. The academy that Lederhosen and Mr. Belushi used to attend gets all the fees plus the deposits."

Now how do you suppose that works?

*Training At The Academy*

The academy, run by 3 women from Australia, that Lederhosen and Mr. Belushi used to attend has a special program for potential "family" members who want to work in Spain, specifically Madrid. They say, "It's a great place. You can live here a long time."

The academy charges a fee so potential family members can begin their Spanish adventure for services they talk about but don't really provide. They told the friend of Lederhosen and Mr. Belushi who was sort-of-sexy long-term housing wasn't a problem. "Good" said the sort-of-sexy friend. "I want to live here for about 2-3 years." In what would have been the first year, the sort-of-sexy friend had to move 5 times.

"I've fulfilled my obligation" the rental agent with the long legs who happened to be the one the academy uses to find housing for potential family members said. "I work hard for you finding you apartments that are undependable, but say I will find you a place and I do, contract filled! If people want to change their mind and don't want you there anymore, I don't protect you. I don't have to because I find the apartment like I said. I have a right to your money. I have a right to steal it and split it with the academy because that's what we do."

"The story she tells about your money being stolen is different from what you say" the 3 Australian women who run the academy said to the sort-of-sexy friend of Lederhosen and Mr. Belushi . "So you'll have to prove everything." "She broke her contract with me", the sort-of-sexy friend replied. "I can prove it."

No one answered her email.

*Newsflash: Mr. Belushi Deported (not Departed, Deported)*

When Mr. Belushi was deported for being a teacher in Madrid with no paperwork, the academy held a special meeting with their other teachers-graduates-students whom they told could live in this great place for a long time. "Don't worry, no one minds especially the government, but if anyone, especially law enforcement people ask, say you're a tourist," they said. After the meeting, the owners of the academy went back to teleconferencing to drum up business.

*Lederhosen and Mr. Belushi In The Teleconferencing Business*

"Yes you can come to this great place and live here a long time. Your Spanish Aventure awaits you", they both said to the people from the Land of the Free. "Don't worry about paperwork, you don't need any. Keep your receipts to prove you've lived here and apply for paperwork yourself if you like." Lederhosen and Mr. Belushi (he came back after 3 months) left out the other part about he and the other teachers being deported.

"We can get you a sim card (that you can get by yourself), we can help you get a bank account (that you can do on your own) and, the best part, we find jobs for you (that you can apply for on your own and be hired without our help – they're listed in the free newspaper that's written in English). Don't forget we help you find housing (that you can find on your own and are better off if you do too). All of this is yours for an agency fee of €360. (We use this number because we keep running you in circles and our help gets you nowhere.) Our academy arranges interviews with one associate who speaks no English at all, another who can't hire you unless you're an EU member, and two more who speak English, might hire you but can't give you that much work.

Come one, come all people from the Land of the Free. We want you! (And your money too!) If the rental agent with long legs doesn't give your deposit back, just accept it and move on."

### *Food For Thought*

The older friend who was sort-of-sexy reflected back on all her Spanish adventures that had been taking place for almost a year now. Can any good come from lies? Had she heard any truth over the past year? "The last dictator had died about 40 years ago and the government said, 'That's it! Now we're a democracy!' But, not everyone can let go that easily. Even people from other lands who moved to Madrid to exploit its vulnerable and volatile state can't put their finger on when, exactly, their perspective changed" the sort-of-sexy older friend of Lederhosen and Mr. Belushi mused to herself. "Maybe it just wasn't so much of a change for them to begin with."

### *Just a Little More Food*

One of the things the sort-of-sexy friend noticed about the people of Madrid was how they were very unaware of each other. Just like little robots. they walk into each other, bump into each other, and step on each other always in a hurry for something.

One day, the sort-of-sexy friend took the train. The train stopped and the doors opened but the people waiting on the platform were in the way. The people on the train were squeezing through them trying to get off. At the same time the sort-of-sexy friend tried to step off, the people on the platform began to push their way into the train, and she noticed she was being pushed back into a seat. Not being certain what to do exactly, she invoked the name of the Lord quite loudly.

The people stopped trying to enter the train and looked around confused. For a moment the sort-of-sexy friend thought they were going to genuflect. Everyone stood back and she disembarked. The same thing happened a second time she was trying to get off the train.

After a little more then a year in Madrid, it occurred to her people who are trying not to follow the way things were anymore need something else to do to distract them and help them look forward to a new outlook.

This was originally intended for ***"An Apartment In Madrid: Chapter 19***" but wasn't included. Here it is:

***Battles Rage On The Back Burner Of My Mind***

Sitting, staring at the wall in the early A.M.
Fighting death trying to take my soul
I wish things could be accepting
At the end of the rope
What more, what else can I do?

I came here with hope so positive
So plenty, something will open up
There's something there for you she'd said
But family never knew
Their advice was never true

When things are falling apart, I saw it posted
They're really falling right into place
I hope so I wrote, it doesn't feel like it, no
Joy has left me in a far cornered space without sun
Without a face

Where to now
I feel worn as if I am done
I spoke with my Grandma and with my dearest friend
I know they are there too
I said, "Remind Him for me, don't ever forget"
At a loss, what is left I can do?

*Epilogue For Lederhosen and Mr. Belushi*

The older friend of Lederhosen and Mr. Belushi who was sort-of-sexy was nicely buzzed after imbibing some Licor de Avellano and milk; after all, milk is good for your bones especially if you're a woman, and the Licor costs only €2,55. She was considering if she should keep noting this and that about the past year in Madrid or not. Nah! This about covers it.

When the sort-of-sexy friend had heard Mr. Belushi was allowed back into the country she thought, "Well, that's Spain's problem."

*On A Day Before Sort-Of-Sexy Left Town*

What can I write to dry up this pen? Nothing, that's great. Found O'Neil's - music good but the menu is overrun with things made with meat. What now? Don't like guacamole; don't want to develop a taste for it. I figured it out. It's possible to get taco salad meatless, it doesn't upset the universe all that much and they're happy to charge the same price. Life can be good.

*Epilogue For The Sort-Of-Sexy Friend*

Time to board the plane. Ciao, ciao!

# Other Publications

***"An Apartment In Madrid : Now in paperback and eBook version for sale at Amazon.com, Booktango.com, Scribd, Kobo, Google and other venues books and eBooks are sold.***

"An Apartment In Madrid", is about life as a teacher living and holding down jobs in Spain and the surrounding adventures, some pretty hair-raising, while on the quest of becoming part of a new culture. It is an unexpected-from-the-inside-out look at teaching abroad, and runs the gamut from excitement, intrigue, success, surprise, wonder, bewilderment, and determination, to incredulity, loss, stress, exhaustion and relief. It's intense, emotional and non-stop.

Who knew the life of an English teacher could be this full of intrigue… Maggie certainly didn't."

Made in the USA
Charleston, SC
29 April 2016